Storybook Collection

DISNEY PRESS

Los Angeles · New York

Contents

"Wanted: Flynn Rider" written by Rebecca L. Schmidt. Copyright © 2015 Disney Enterprises, Inc.

"The Perfect Pearl" written by Elle D. Riscoe. Copyright © 2014 Disney Enterprises, Inc.

"Merida's Wild Ride" written by Susan Amerikaner. Copyright © 2013 Disney Enterprises, Inc.

"The Secret of the Star Shell" adapted by Meredith Rusu from the original story "The Shimmering Star Necklace," written by Gail Herman, originally published by Disney Press. Copyright © 2012 Disney Enterprises, Inc.

"The Best Beignet" written by Calliope Glass. Copyright © 2015 Disney Enterprises, Inc.

"The Great Jewel Hunt" written by Kitty Richards. Copyright © 2014 Disney Enterprises, Inc.

"A New Mouse" written by Calliope Glass. Copyright © 2013 Disney Enterprises, Inc.

"The Sweetest Day Ever" written by Brittany Candau. Copyright © 2015 Disney Enterprises, Inc.

"A New Chef in Town" written by Hannah Eliot. Copyright © 2015 Disney Enterprises, Inc.

"The Legend of the Emeralds" adapted by Hannah Eliot from the original story written by Ellie O'Ryan. Copyright © 2013 Disney Enterprises, Inc.

"Ariel and the Whale Song" adapted by Hannah Eliot from the original story "Ariel and the Big Baby," written by Amy Sky Koster. Copyright © 2015 Disney Enterprises, Inc.

"The Search for the Sultan's Stone" written by Hannah Eliot. Copyright © 2015 Disney Enterprises, Inc.

"The Heart of a Champion" adapted from the book *More 5-Minute Princess Stories*, written by Lara Bergen. Copyright © 2007 Disney Enterprises, Inc.

"Khan to the Rescue" written by Calliope Glass. Copyright © 2015 Disney Enterprises, Inc.

"Tiana and Charlotte's Friendship Fix-up" written by Cynthea Liu. Copyright © 2015 Disney Enterprises, Inc.

"A Little Mischief" written by Rebecca L. Schmidt. Copyright © 2015 Disney Enterprises, Inc.

"The Friendship Invention" adapted by Meredith Rusu from the original story written by Amy Sky Koster. Copyright © 2015 Disney Enterprises, Inc.

"A Moment to Remember" written by Catherine McCafferty and originally published in *Happily Ever After Stories*. Copyright © 2007 Disney Enterprises, Inc.

"Ariel's Royal Wedding" written by Apple Jordan. Copyright © 2013 Disney Enterprises, Inc.

Unless otherwise noted, all illustrations by the Disney Storybook Art Team.

Collection copyright © 2015 Disney Enterprises, Inc.

For information address Disney Press, 1101 Flower Street, Glendale, California 91201.

Printed in the United States of America

Fourth Edition, September 2015

10 9 8 7 6 5 4 3 2 1

G942-9090-6-15226

Library of Congress Control Number: 2015936486

ISBN 978-1-4847-1283-2

For more Disney Press fun, visit www.disneybooks.com

Tangled

Wanted: Flynn Rider

Princess Rapunzel and Flynn Rider were visiting their friends at the Snuggly Duckling. Rapunzel was learning how to play the piano from Hook Hand. Flynn was learning interior design. He was less excited than Rapunzel.

"A little to the right," Gunther said.

"The right? Really?" Flynn asked as he moved a vase.

Suddenly, the door flew open. It was the noble horse Max, followed by two royal guards. Max sadly held up a WANTED poster in his mouth. It had a picture of Flynn!

"Anyone else getting a sense of déjà vu?" Flynn asked.

"It looks like they think you stole my tiara again," Rapunzel said as she read the warrant for Flynn's arrest.

"What? I didn't do anything! Why does everyone always think it's me?" Flynn said.

Rapunzel just looked at him.

"Well, I guess they might have a few reasons," Flynn said.

The guards explained that late the night before, someone who looked just like Flynn had sneaked into the castle and stolen Rapunzel's tiara, right from underneath the guards' noses! There were witnesses all over town who said they had seen Flynn running away from the scene of the crime. The guards had no choice but to arrest Flynn.

"Don't worry," Rapunzel said. "We'll clear this whole thing up. You'll be back to interior designing in no time."

"Hurry," Flynn said as the guards led him away. "And don't let Gunther move the vase!"

The door shut behind Max, the guards, and Flynn.

"What are we going to do?" Hook Hand asked Rapunzel.

Rapunzel looked at all her friends in the Snuggly Duckling. She was worried. She knew Flynn hadn't stolen the tiara, but she would have to prove it. "Let's go back to town. It's time to investigate!" Rapunzel said.

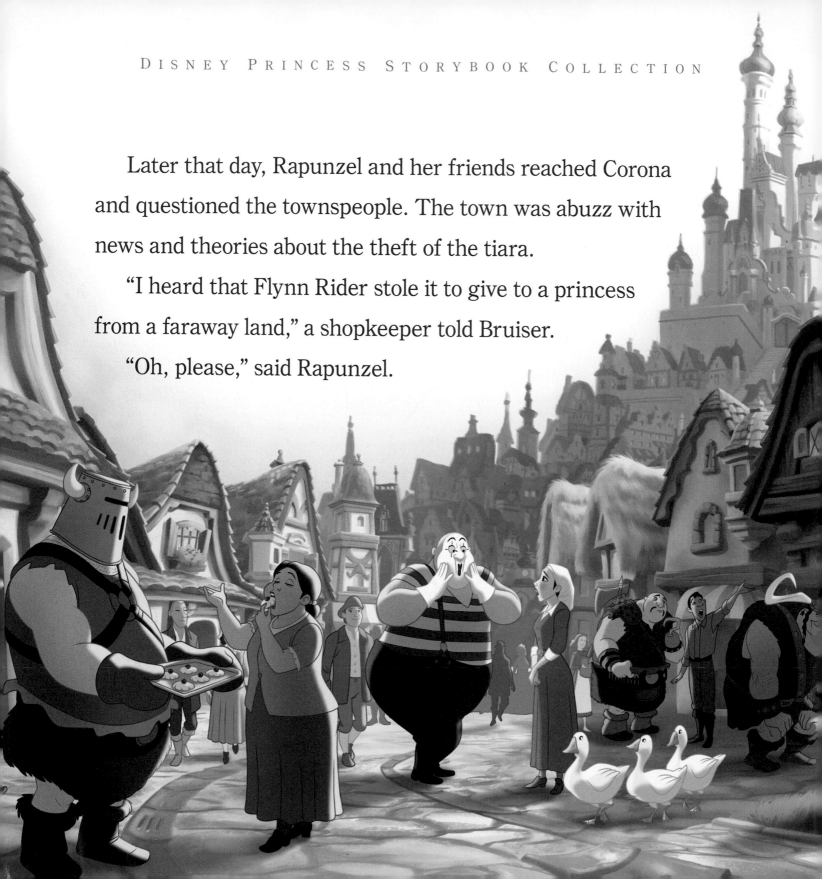

Later that day, Rapunzel and her friends reached Corona and questioned the townspeople. The town was abuzz with news and theories about the theft of the tiara.

"I heard that Flynn Rider stole it to give to a princess from a faraway land," a shopkeeper told Bruiser.

"Oh, please," said Rapunzel.

A baker said that he had heard Flynn was trading the tiara for his freedom from an evil magician. And a gardener said that Flynn was going to use the tiara to buy a ship and sail far, far away.

"He'd never do that," Rapunzel said. "He hates sailing."

Many people swore they had seen Flynn the night before. The librarian had spotted Flynn sneaking around by the paint shop. A sailor was sure he'd seen Flynn down by the docks.

"But how did you know it was him?" Rapunzel asked the sailor.

"The thief was wearing a green vest, just like Flynn always wears," the sailor said matter-of-factly. "Besides, he's stolen the tiara before."

"But he couldn't have been at the paint shop *and* the docks. They're on opposite sides of town, and there aren't two Flynns," Rapunzel said. "Plus, the last time he stole the tiara, he had help. . . ."

Rapunzel turned to her friends. She was starting to suspect who might *really* be behind the theft. But to clear Flynn's name, they would have to catch the true criminals.

"I think I have a plan," Rapunzel said, drawing everyone into a tight huddle. "Now, listen closely. . . ."

Rapunzel and her friends rushed to the castle to tell the King and Queen her plan.

"First I need the royal messengers to tell the town we're moving all the royal jewels to the throne room to protect them," Rapunzel said. "Then I need you to send Max and all his guards on an important mission out of town."

"But then everyone will know that the castle and all the jewels are undefended!" said the King and Queen together.

"Exactly." Rapunzel smiled.

The sun began to set, and the townspeople watched in amazement as Max led all his guards out of the city gates.

"They must be going to find the princess's tiara!" the gardener told the town librarian.

The royal messengers told everyone that the kingdom's jewels had all been moved to the castle's throne room. With everything in one place, the precious treasure would be easier to protect.

"Especially from evil magicians," the baker told the gardener.

Soon it was time for everyone in the castle to go to sleep. It had been a long, eventful day, and everyone was tired. Without any of the guards in the castle, there was no one to notice two shadowy figures crawling over the roof. And there were no guards to see those same two figures lower a rope into the dark throne room and slowly climb down. The thieves were back to steal the royal jewels!

The two people softly landed on the floor of the throne room. They quietly walked toward the center of the room, looking for the royal jewels. But the room was empty!

"I don't understand," said a gruff voice. "Where are all the jewels?"

Suddenly, the room was full of light. Rapunzel and her friends ran out of hiding. It had been a trap all along!

In the harsh light of her lantern, Rapunzel saw that the figures were dressed in matching green vests—just like Flynn's. But she wasn't fooled for a moment. As Atilla and Hook Hand restrained the criminals, Rapunzel removed their brown wigs to reveal . . . the Stabbington brothers!

"How did you know we'd be here?" the Stabbington brothers asked Rapunzel.

"I knew that the idea of getting more jewels would be too tempting for you to pass up," Rapunzel said. "Especially when you had seen all the guards leave the city. You didn't know that I had a scary group of thugs to help me out!"

Rapunzel explained to her friends how the Stabbington brothers had disguised themselves as Flynn to hide their true identities. That was why the townspeople had seen Flynn in so many different places. There *had* been two of him!

"We knew that you would get to the bottom of this, Rapunzel," the Queen said, giving her daughter a hug.

Rapunzel smiled. "Now, if you'll excuse me, I have some business in the dungeon. . . ."

With Flynn's name cleared, Max and Rapunzel personally freed him from jail.

"I left the room warm for you," Flynn told the Stabbington brothers as Hook Hand and Vladamir locked them up.

Now there was only one mystery left to solve. "Where is my tiara?" Rapunzel asked the Stabbington brothers. "I can get my frying pan if I have to!"

"Boys, I'd be careful," Flynn said. "You do not want to be on the wrong end of Rapunzel's frying pan. Believe me. I know."

"It's right here!" said one of the brothers, pulling the tiara from beneath his vest. "After we stole all the jewels, we were planning to go to the docks and sail away to a faraway land."

"Not anymore," Flynn said as he took the tiara and placed it on Rapunzel's head. "That's better."

To celebrate solving the mystery, everyone went back to the Snuggly Duckling for a "Welcome Back" party.

"Be honest, you were a little nervous," Rapunzel said to Flynn.

"Me? Nervous? Never! I'm Flynn Rider. I've sailed to distant lands to see fair princesses and battled evil magicians. Adventure is my life!" Flynn said with a wink.

"Good thing, too," Gunther said. "Because you're a terrible interior designer."

Rapunzel laughed. It was good to be among friends.

Beauty and the Beast

The Perfect Pearl

It was a lazy afternoon at the Beast's castle, and Belle and Chip were exploring the library. The Beast had just given Belle all the books for her very own, and Belle hoped that someday she would read every single one.

"What do you suppose is behind these doors, Chip?" Belle asked the enchanted teacup.

"Books!" Chip replied.

Belle laughed. "I meant what *kind* of books, silly."

Belle threw open the doors. "I knew it. More beautiful adventures—tucked away and forgotten, maybe even unread!" she said.

It wasn't that the Beast didn't use the library. But when he did, he always read the same book.

"My library is your library," he liked to remind Belle. "Read and enjoy any book you find."

It hadn't been long since Belle had agreed to stay at the castle in return for her father's freedom. But each day she was getting to know the Beast better. She was starting to think that he might care about her happiness.

So Belle took the Beast at his word and made
herself at home in the library. Many days she spent
hours there, reading book after book, losing all track of time.

Belle considered books priceless
treasures. So when she took a break
from reading, she gave the books
special attention. Belle asked
Babette to help her dust them. She
shelved any stray books. She even
pressed flat any folded pages.

One morning, Belle noticed the Beast had left his favorite book lying open on the arm of his chair. "That's not good for the binding," Belle said.

She picked up the book and examined it. Although the leather cover was worn, it was a beautiful volume with a brass clasp decorated with pearls. But Belle noticed one of the pearls was missing!

Belle looked around on the floor, in case it had fallen out just then. Chip helped her search. "I found something!" he called.

There by the library door was a single perfect pearl.

"Let's see if it fits," Belle suggested. She dropped the pearl into the hole in the clasp.

"It's perfect!" said Chip.

But the pearl was loose and wouldn't stay put.

"I have an idea," Belle said. "This book is obviously the Beast's favorite. I'll fix it up a bit at a time. As the finishing touch, I'll reattach the pearl."

"Then you can surprise him!" Chip cried.

Belle nodded. She was happy to do something nice for the Beast.

Belle got right to work. She borrowed some rags and polish
from Mrs. Potts and gently cleaned the leather cover. Then she put
the book back on the Beast's chair so he wouldn't miss it.

But when the Beast came into the library, he didn't pick up his book. He seemed to be looking for something.

"Can I help?" Belle asked.

"NO!" he bellowed. Then, more quietly, he added, "I mean, no. Excuse me." Without another word, he left the room.

Belle was surprised but shrugged it off, assuming the Beast's bad mood would pass. At least this time he had apologized for his rude behavior.

That afternoon, Belle did some more work on the book. Carefully, she smoothed out rumpled pages and polished the brass clasp.

"I can see myself!" Chip exclaimed.

Again Belle put the book back in its place on the Beast's chair.

Later that evening, Belle passed the Beast in the hall. She smiled and stopped to greet him. "Good evening—"

"Good night!" he snapped, hurrying by.

Belle stood there, a bit stunned. He hadn't even glanced her way. *Is something the matter?* she wondered.

The next morning, it was time for Belle to add the pearl. But she wasn't sure she was ready to give the book to the Beast. He had been so grouchy the day before. *What will he be like today?* she wondered.

Just then, the Beast burst through the door. "You?" he cried. "You've had the pearl all along? I've been looking everywhere trying to find it!"

"Well, why didn't you say so!" Belle shouted. Then she tossed the pearl onto the table. "By the way, I've been fixing up your book as a surprise."

The Beast was shocked. He looked at the book. He picked up the pearl. Then he smiled—and began to laugh.

Belle stormed toward the door.

"Belle, wait," the Beast said. His gentle voice made Belle stop and turn. "I've been working on something for you, too."

In the Beast's hand was a lovely antique pin. "It's been in my family a long time," he explained. "I wanted you to have it. But first, I had something to add."

He placed the pearl on the pin, at the base of the rose. It fit perfectly.

"I removed the pearl from my book yesterday," he said. "But I must have dropped it on my way out and—" He looked down. "I'm sorry I blamed you."

Now it was Belle's turn to laugh. "Well, I'm sorry I stole your surprise."

Belle pinned the gold rose with the perfect pearl to her dress. Then she watched as the Beast noticed his book's shining brass clasp, polished cover, and smooth pages.

"Thank you, Belle," he said. "You've made it new."

Belle and the Beast still had much to learn about each other. But their hearts were in the right place.

BRAVE
Merida's Wild Ride

It was a soggy, stormy afternoon. Merida sat in the stables reading from an old book of Highland tales. She and her horse, Angus, wanted to go for a ride—if only the weather would clear up.

"Look at this picture of a brownie," Merida said. "The book says they're little goblins who cause mischief unless you keep them well fed. Sounds like my brothers. . . ."

Angus snorted, shaking his head. It was clear that he wanted nothing to do with magical creatures, especially after their last encounter. Even though Merida had been able to transform her mum back from a bear to a human, Merida had learned that magic was not to be taken lightly.

Merida read on until the raindrops slowed and the clouds began to scatter.

"Come, lad," said Merida to Angus. "The sun's breaking through. Let's go for a ride."

They galloped across the bridge and down the hill. But just as they reached the woods, Merida saw a flash of gray dart through the trees. "What was that?" she cried.

But Angus didn't want to follow it—whatever it was.

"Don't be a ninny," Merida chided him. "I'm sure it's not a bear." But what was it? Merida guided Angus into the woods, keeping her eyes open for another glimpse of the creature.

As they rode, Merida kept catching flashes of the animal. She urged Angus to go faster until they broke through the trees and into a clearing. There stood a magnificent gray horse. Its coat shimmered. Its mane was like fine silk.

Breathless with excitement, Merida whispered to Angus, "He's beautiful."

Merida dismounted and approached the horse with a gentle smile. "Come here. I won't hurt you."

Suddenly, Angus blocked Merida's path.

"Angus," she called,
"don't be jealous, lad!
This horse must be lost.
We need to help him—
make sure he's safe."

Merida cooed to the gray horse, and it responded with a soft whinny.

"See, Angus? He's friendly." Merida stroked the new horse's nose playfully. "Now I'll ride him back to the castle, and you follow close behind. Okay, Angus?"

Merida had a spare bridle in Angus's pack, but she decided not to use it. She didn't want to spook the horse with unfamiliar reins. Instead, Merida decided she could guide him with her hands wrapped in his mane.

Angus gave a resigned snort as Merida swung up onto the gray horse's back. But as soon as she mounted him, the horse reared wildly.

Merida tried to calm the horse, but he started running. Faster and faster, the strange horse galloped until the field was far behind them. Soon the trees began to thin, and Merida gasped in horror. They were racing toward the edge of a cliff!

Merida tried everything she could to get the horse to stop, but nothing worked! She realized her only choice was to leap from the horse's back. But when she moved to jump, her hands were stuck to the horse's mane. His hair wasn't sticky or knotted, yet Merida could not free her hands. It was as if they were held there by magic.

Merida tried to
slide off the side of
the horse, but nothing
could free her hands
from his mane. She
thought she was out of
options. Then, suddenly,
the runaway horse
brushed against the
trunk of a tree. Trapped
rainwater fell down around
Merida. Effortlessly, one of her hands came loose.

But Merida's other hand was still stuck. Merida did the only
thing she could think of.

"Angus!" she cried. "Help!" Merida could only hope that her
friend had heard her cry.

Merida looked up at the sound of a whinny. Angus galloped up next to them—and he was carrying the spare bridle in his mouth! He must have pulled it from his pack to help Merida.

Angus tossed it through the air just as they were nearing the cliff's edge. Merida caught it with her free hand and slipped it over the horse's head. As soon as the horse was bridled, Merida's trapped hand came free. With the reins, she turned the horse away from the steep drop-off.

Now that the horse had calmed down, Merida guided him to a safe path beside the sea. As they reached the shore, the horse finally slowed to a stop. Grateful, Merida jumped off.

The stallion stood quietly. Merida looked in his eyes for an answer about what had caused the wild ride. It was clear to her that this was no ordinary horse. It must be a creature of magic.

Merida removed the bridle and whispered quietly, "What are you?"

But the horse did not reply. He simply moved his head softly, as if he was nodding, before galloping down the misty shoreline and into the water.

Merida frowned as she watched him. As the horse raced deeper into the sea, he seemed to disappear into fog.

Merida mounted Angus and returned home. She was glad that the strange horse had not harmed her, but she wanted an explanation for her wild ride.

Back at the stable, Merida flipped through the book of Highland legends, looking for answers, until she saw a picture of a very familiar horse.

"Look!" she showed the book to Angus. "It's a kelpie. The book says 'Once a bridle is put on a kelpie, the water horse will do your bidding.'"

Angus snorted in disbelief.

"Don't worry, lad," Merida said. "I won't be riding another one any time soon. You're the only horse for me."

Angus nuzzled his head against Merida's hand as if to reply that she was the only girl for him.

THE LITTLE MERMAID
The Secret of the Star Shell

"Do, re, mi, fa, so, la, ti, do!"

"Very good, Laurel!" Princess Ariel applauded.

It was a bright and sunny morning in the village. Ariel was giving her young friend Laurel a singing lesson.

"Why don't we try this one next?" Ariel pointed to a song in her music book.

Laurel's eyes sparkled. "'The Song of the Sea.' That reminds me of my new best friend!"

"What's your friend's name?" Ariel asked.

Laurel suddenly hesitated. "Um, I'm not sure you'd know her. But we love playing together." She glanced at the clock. "I'm meeting her right after our lesson. Maybe I'll sing 'The Song of the Sea' for her, too!"

52

Later that afternoon, Ariel visited her sisters by the ocean.

"Ariel!" Adella sang out. "We brought you a present!"

She handed Ariel a shimmering shell shaped like a star. It had a delicate ribbon tied to the top.

"It's beautiful!" Ariel gasped. "Where did you find it?"

"It was caught in the current," Adella explained. "It's a star shell. It's supposed to grant wishes!"

Ariel looked at her sisters excitedly. "Shall we try it?"

They each took turns making one wish, but nothing happened.

"That's all right," Ariel said. She tied the ribbon around her neck to wear the shell like a necklace. "It's a beautiful gift. Now I'll carry a part of the sea wherever I go."

As Ariel walked back to the village, she passed Laurel's cottage. Suddenly, Laurel's father, Mr. Hansen, came running out.

"Princess Ariel! Is Laurel with you?" He sounded upset.

"No," said Ariel. "Has something happened?"

"Laurel went to play with a friend after your music lesson, but she never came back," Mr. Hansen explained. "I checked with all her school friends. Laurel isn't with any of them. I hope she hasn't gotten lost."

"Laurel mentioned that she'd made a new friend," Ariel said. "Maybe they're still playing and they lost track of time. Perhaps there's a clue in her room about who this friend is and where we could find her?"

Together, they checked the girl's room. Scattered on Laurel's desk were school drawings and a pink journal open to an entry:

Dear Diary,

I met a new friend by the ocean. Her name is Calista! We've played together every day this week. She even gave me a beautiful necklace. Calista said not to tell anyone about our secret friendship. But that's okay—it's fun having a secret friend. I'm going to buy her a treat from the pastry shop!

Ariel and Mr. Hansen agreed to split up and search for Laurel. Mr. Hansen went to ask the village parents if they knew Calista. Ariel hurried to the pastry shop.

"Hmmm," the baker said, when Ariel explained what had happened. "Yes, I do remember Laurel stopping by. She wanted seaweed puffs! Can you imagine?"

Just then, a little girl named Maggie bounded into the bakery with her mother. She handed the baker a colorful card.

He smiled. "Why, it's a thank-you note!"

"It was part of a school assignment," Maggie's mother said. "Miss Toft asked the students to write them, and Maggie wanted to thank you for her birthday cake."

Ariel looked thoughtful. Miss Toft was Laurel's teacher, too. That meant Laurel would have had the same assignment. Perhaps she wrote a thank-you note to Calista for the necklace, and it would hold another clue!

At the school, the teacher was happy to show Ariel the thank-you notes. Laurel's was written on a bright yellow card.

Dear Princess Ariel,

Thank you for helping me practice singing.

Your friend, Laurel

"Oh, dear." Ariel sighed. The card was lovely, but it certainly wasn't a clue.

"Laurel loves drawing," the teacher said. "Just yesterday, I asked my students to make a picture of their best friend. Laurel couldn't wait to get started."

"Best friend?" Ariel exclaimed. "Maybe she drew a picture of Calista!"

Miss Toft took Ariel to Laurel's desk. "Surely the picture is in here somewhere."

After looking through a few folders, Ariel found a picture labeled MY BEST FRIEND.

Two girls were in the drawing. One was Laurel, with short brown hair. And the other girl had wavy blond hair. It had to be Calista.

And she was a mermaid.

Ariel thanked Miss Toft and ran back to Mr. Hansen's home.

Mr. Hansen looked up hopefully when he spotted Ariel. "Princess! None of the parents knew a Calista. Did you have better luck?"

"Yes!" Ariel exclaimed. She quickly told Mr. Hansen what she had discovered.

"Could Calista really be a mermaid?" Mr. Hansen asked.

"It does make sense," Ariel said. "Look at the clues. Laurel met her by the ocean. She tried to buy her seaweed puffs. And Calista wanted to keep their friendship a secret. She must be a mermaid!"

"But then where is my daughter?" Mr. Hansen asked.

Ariel smiled. "I think I know just how to find out!"

Ariel led Mr. Hansen to the beach and called for her friends Sebastian and Flounder. Ariel asked them to fetch her father, King Triton, so he could transform her back into a mermaid. In no time at all, Ariel was searching for Calista under the sea.

After asking the merfolk, Ariel and her father found Calista's family's grotto.

The young mermaid was there. And she was very nervous.

"You're not in trouble," Ariel assured Calista. "We just want to know where Laurel is. Her father is very worried."

"I don't want anyone to worry," Calista said softly. She led Ariel and Triton to her bedroom.

"It's all right," Calista called. "You can come out."

Slowly, Laurel swam out from under Calista's bed.

Ariel gasped. "Laurel! You're here! And . . . you're a mermaid, too?"

"It's so hard to explain." Laurel sniffled. "When I went to see Calista this morning, I was wearing my star shell necklace. As we were splashing in the water, I told Calista that I wished I could play with her under the ocean for real. All of a sudden, my necklace lit up. And I turned into a mermaid!"

Calista nodded. "We realized the shell must be magical. So we thought we could just wish Laurel to be human again later."

"But while we were playing on the octopus slide," Laurel said, "my necklace got swept away in a current. I didn't know what to do!"

Suddenly, Calista spotted Ariel's star shell necklace. "Oh, Princess! You found it! That means we can wish Laurel human again!"

Ariel looked to her father. King Triton smiled kindly.

"I'm afraid the Legend of the Star Shell works a little differently," he said. "Come with me to the surface, and I'll explain."

At the surface, King Triton held up the star shell. It glittered in the sunlight.

"Star shells can only grant one wish," he said. "In order to undo the wish, the shell must be broken."

Calista turned to Laurel. "When you're human again, will you still visit me by the ocean?"

"Of course!" Laurel said with a smile.

Together, everyone swam back to shore. Then Ariel handed Laurel the star shell. "It's up to you now."

Laurel lifted the shell high up in the air, paused, and then brought it down against a large flat rock. In a burst of light, her mermaid tail changed back into legs.

"I'm human!" Laurel cried. She hugged Calista tightly. "It was a wonderful adventure. We'll still see each other all the time. I promise."

Immediately, Mr. Hansen rushed over. "Laurel! Thank goodness you're safe!"

"Oh, Daddy!" Laurel cried. "I have so much to tell you."

A few days later, Ariel asked Calista and Laurel to meet her by the water.

"I have presents for you both," Ariel said. She handed the girls two brand-new necklaces made from star shell pieces.

"They're beautiful!" Laurel breathed.

"Thank you, Princess Ariel," Calista said.

Ariel smiled. "When I was wearing the star shell, it was like carrying a part of the ocean with me. Now you two can always carry a piece of your adventure with you wherever you go."

THE PRINCESS AND THE FROG
The Best Beignet

Early one morning, Tiana was pulling a tray of cornbread out of the oven when her best friend, Charlotte, burst into the kitchen.

"I have some big news for you," Charlotte told Tiana dramatically. "You'd better sit down."

Tiana sat down.

"The World Beignet Championships are being held in Paris this year!" Charlotte said. "And we simply must go!"

"The World Beignet Championships?" Tiana asked, shaking her head. She'd never heard of the event, but it sounded amazing. The only thing Tiana loved more than making beignets was eating them.

"Don't worry," Charlotte said, "you're definitely going to win. I already signed you up!"

Tiana fell out of her chair.

"Aaaaand this is why I made sure you were sitting down," Charlotte said.

"Fantastic!" Naveen said when Tiana told him about the championships. "I know you will love Paris! And you make the best beignets I've ever had, so you're sure to win!"

Tiana blushed. She knew she was a terrific baker, but it was nice to hear Naveen say it.

"Europe, here we come!" Naveen said happily.

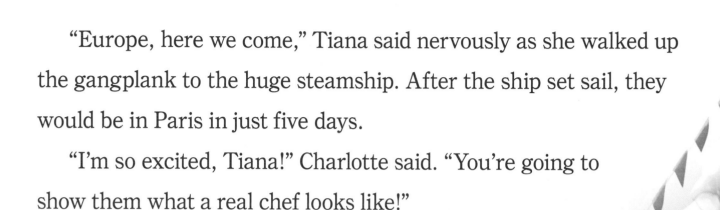

"Europe, here we come," Tiana said nervously as she walked up the gangplank to the huge steamship. After the ship set sail, they would be in Paris in just five days.

"I'm so excited, Tiana!" Charlotte said. "You're going to show them what a real chef looks like!"

"And you'll finally get to see Paris!" Naveen added.

But Tiana didn't have time to see Paris.

"I'm sorry," Tiana said when they got there. "The contest is in three days, and I have to start getting ready right now. I have a lot to do!"

"But there's so much to see!" Naveen protested. "The Louvre Museum! Notre-Dame Cathedral! The Eiffel Tower!"

"You and Charlotte go without me," Tiana said. "I have to be completely prepared for the contest. If I win, it will be huge for the restaurant!"

"Just today!" Charlotte begged. "Just give yourself one day to do something fun! Maybe we can all have a nice lunch in the hotel restaurant."

Tiana sighed. "Okay," she said. "But just tonight. Tomorrow morning I have to get to work."

But the restaurant didn't work out so well.

"Mademoiselles et monsieur," the waiter said, "I present to you our signature dish: frogs' legs."

"Okay, so that was a bad idea," Charlotte said as the trio quickly left the restaurant.

Tiana shuddered. She still remembered what it was like to *be* a frog.

"We can still have some fun!" Naveen said, leading them through the streets of Paris.

"You see?" he said, pointing up as they rounded a corner. "The Eiffel Tower!"

Tiana looked up, and then up and up and up some more. "It's so tall!" she said. She took a step back to get a better view and tumbled right off the curb!

"Ahhh!" Tiana cried as she fell right on her wrist.

"Okay, so that was a bad idea, too," Charlotte said as they left the doctor's office a few hours later.

"I'm so sorry," Naveen said. He hung his head miserably.

"How am I supposed to bake the best beignets in the world with a sprained wrist?" Tiana cried. "Why did we have to have fun today? Oh, I wish I'd never listened to the two of you. If I'd just gone straight to the kitchen, this never would have happened!"

"Tiana," Charlotte said, "we are going to fix this, and you are going to win that contest."

"How?" Tiana asked.

"I have an idea," Charlotte said.

The next morning, Tiana, Charlotte, and Naveen went to talk to the beignet judge.

"You see," Charlotte said, pointing at Tiana's arm, "it was all our fault, so Naveen and I think we should be able to help Tiana in the contest. It's only fair."

"Well," said the judge, "it is a most unusual request. But yes, Tiana, these two may help you in the Beignet Championships."

Tiana breathed a big sigh of relief.

So Tiana got to work teaching Charlotte and Naveen everything she knew about beignets: how to weigh the flour, how to mix the *pâte à choux*, how to test the temperature of the frying oil, and even her secret ingredient. "I add just a pinch of nutmeg to the powdered sugar at the end," Tiana admitted.

"Genius!" Naveen cried.

By the day of the championships, Tiana felt good about their chances. Charlotte was fast with a whisk, and Naveen was good with the fryer.

"Everything is going to be okay," Tiana said to herself nervously as the competition began. Under Tiana's instruction, Charlotte whisked up the beignet dough.

"Perfect!" Tiana said, after taking a small taste. "To the fryer!"

With Naveen's help, the beignets fried up light and airy and perfectly golden. Everything was going well, until—

"No!" Charlotte cried. She'd dropped the nutmeg jar, spilling it all over the floor. "The secret ingredient! I'm so sorry, Tia."

But to Charlotte's surprise, Tiana just laughed. She reached into her pocket and pulled out an extra jar of nutmeg. "You didn't think I'd cook without a backup, did you?"

"Tiana, you crazy overpreparer!" Charlotte shrieked as she hugged Tiana.

"Watch the arm." Tiana smiled through gritted teeth.

"Have I mentioned you're a genius?" Naveen said.

And the judge agreed.

Back at the hotel, Charlotte admired Tiana's first-place trophy.

"I'm so happy you won, Tiana!"

"No," Tiana said, "*we* won. And now, we celebrate!"

"Do you mean—" Naveen started hopefully.

"It's finally time to see Paris," Tiana said, grinning.

Snow White
and the Seven Dwarfs

The Great Jewel Hunt

"Farewell, my love!" said Snow White. The Prince was leaving on a royal trip. It was the first time the newlyweds would be apart.

"I'll be home soon," replied the Prince. "In the meantime, I've left an envelope for you on the well. It's the first clue in a treasure hunt. At the end, you'll find a special gift!"

The clue was in plain sight. The Dwarfs gathered around as Snow White opened the envelope. "I wonder what the gift will be?" she said. Then she read the clue aloud:

Can't leave you a kiss,
Or even a hug,
So here is a clue:
Look under the . . .

"I know!" cried Sneezy. "The Prince left the next clue under a bug!" Sneezy quickly led everyone to the garden.

Snow White and the Dwarfs looked under ladybugs, spiders, butterflies, beetles, and, very carefully, bumblebees. But they didn't find a thing.

"Actually, it would be pretty hard to hide a clue under a bug," said Snow White. "Maybe it's hidden under something that sounds like *bug*?"

"Under a jug?" suggested Happy.

"No, he must have meant under a mug!" said Grumpy. "To the kitchen!"

But as the Dwarfs searched inside, Grumpy tripped over Dopey.

"Crawling on the floor in someone's castle is mad banners," scolded Doc. "I mean, it's bad manners!"

"Whatever are you doing, Dopey?" asked Snow White.

Dopey crawled out from under the carpet and held up an envelope.

Snow White clapped her hands with excitement. "Under the *rug*! Oh, Dopey, you're a genius!"

Snow White read the clue:

Hooray, you found it! Easy when you try.
Now in the kitchen, just lift up the . . .

"Pie!" shouted all of the Dwarfs at the same time. Searching had given them quite an appetite!

Sure enough, the next clue was hidden underneath the pie plate! First Snow White served everyone a big piece of freshly baked gooseberry pie. Then, while they were eating, she read the next clue.

Put on a smile, it's no time to frown.
You'll find the next clue in your royal . . .

Snow White thought for a moment. "My royal gown?" she guessed. The Dwarfs all nodded in agreement and quickly finished off their pie.

In Snow White's
dressing room, the Dwarfs
searched through gown after
gown after gown. But there was
no clue to be found.

"Now we'll never find Snow White's gift," Sneezy said sadly.

Grumpy noticed Bashful standing in the corner. "Why aren't
you searching?" Grumpy asked him.

"Why, he doesn't have to," Snow White said. "He's wearing my
royal crown. That must be where the clue is!"

Bashful took off the crown . . .

. . . and inside was the clue!

The gift is almost yours.
My, my, this game has flown!
There's one thing left to do:
Go look upon your . . .

"Stone!" offered Sneezy.

"That's silly," said
Grumpy. "It must be bone!"

Soon all of the Dwarfs
were shouting out their own
ideas.

"Cone!"

"Cologne!"

"Trombone!"

As the Dwarfs
guessed, Snow White
realized someone was
missing. "Where's Sleepy?" she asked.
They all set off to look for him. But he wasn't in the
dining room. Or in the kitchen. Or in the Great Hall.

Snow White was starting to get worried, when she
heard a shout from the Royal Throne Room.

"I found him!" Happy cried.

Sleepy was sound asleep on Snow White's throne.

"That's the answer to the clue," she whispered. "'Go look upon your throne.'"

"So where's the gift?" Grumpy grumped.

"Right there," said Doc. "Look!"

Sitting at the very top of Snow White's throne were two birds holding something that sparkled.

To everyone's surprise, the birds flew down and placed a
delicate necklace around Snow White's neck. The gift was a
stunning heart-shaped ruby on a golden chain.

"Why, it's the color of love," she said.

Doc saw that Snow White was holding something else.
"The birds left a note!" he cried.

Snow White opened the envelope and read aloud:

Yes, jewels are lovely,
But as this hunt ends,
Keep one thought in mind:
The best gifts are . . .

"Odds and ends,"
said Sneezy.

"No, it's definitely
chickens and hens,"
said Happy.

"Pens?" Bashful
suggested quietly.

Grumpy couldn't believe his ears. "What's wrong with you fellas? The answer is 'friends'!"

"You're right," said Snow White. "I love my new necklace, but the best part of today was the time we spent together. Friends are the greatest gift of all!"

All the Dwarfs cheered. Not even Grumpy could argue with that.

Cinderella

A New Mouse

Warm sunlight streamed through the windows of Cinderella's parlor as she and her mouse friends shared afternoon tea.

Even though the food was delicious, Cinderella found it difficult to enjoy the tasty treats. She was too busy thinking about her friend Gabrielle, who would be visiting very soon. Gabrielle was the Prince's cousin, but she lived so far away that Cinderella didn't get to see her very often.

Just then, a royal page entered the parlor. "Lady Gabrielle has arrived," he announced. Gabrielle swept into the room and ran to hug Cinderella.

"It's so good to see you, dear," she said. As the two friends chatted excitedly, Jaq and Gus noticed that Gabrielle had an unusual item with her.

"What's-a that?" Jaq said. He pointed eagerly to a fancy little house that Gabrielle had set on the floor.

Gabrielle noticed the curious mice and explained right away. "Let me introduce you to my beloved friend Babette." Gabrielle opened the little door to the house, and Babette walked onto her hand.

Jaq and Gus couldn't believe it. Babette was a mouse!

"I found little Babette lost in one of the manor bedrooms," Gabrielle said. "After meeting your mouse friends, Cinderella, I just knew I had to take her in."

Jaq and Gus waved to the new mouse, but Babette just stared at them.

"Would you like a crumpet, Babette?" Cinderella asked.

The mouse took a piece and ran back onto Gabrielle's hand.

"She should-a said 'thank-a you,'" Jaq whispered to Gus.

"Rude!" Gus agreed.

"Cinderella, dear, you simply must show me the castle garden," Gabrielle said, setting down Babette.

"Jaq, Gus, perhaps you can give Babette a tour of the castle," Cinderella suggested.

Jaq and Gus agreed and immediately began showing Babette all their favorite places in the castle.

"This-a the library!" Jaq said.

"Lots-a books," Gus said, pointing.

Babette looked around but didn't say a word.

Then Jaq and Gus took Babette to the grand ballroom. "You have a ballroom?" Jaq asked, trying to start a conversation.

Babette nodded. And that was all.

Jaq and Gus took Babette all over the castle, hoping to find something that she would be interested in. But no matter where they went, Babette just nodded or stayed silent.

That evening, Cinderella asked Jaq and Gus how their day with Babette had been.

"She's a snob," Jaq told Cinderella.

"Stuck up!" Gus agreed.

"Now, now," Cinderella said gently. "You hardly know her. Give her a chance."

As Cinderella set the pair of mice down on the ground, she noticed something was missing. "My bracelet!" she gasped. "It must have fallen off during Gabrielle's tour."

"We can find it, Cinderelly!" Jaq said.

"Oh, thank you for offering," Cinderella said, "but we went all over the castle. The bracelet could be anywhere."

"No problem for Jaq and Gus-Gus!" Jaq said proudly. "Follow us, Cinderelly!"

They went to ask Gabrielle about the last time she remembered seeing the bracelet.

"Oh, dear. I'm afraid I was so busy admiring the castle that I wasn't paying much attention to Cinderella's bracelet," Gabrielle said.

"I can help you look," a soft voice said. It was Babette, stepping out from her little house.

Jaq and Gus looked suspiciously at Babette, but Cinderella spoke up for her. "That would be wonderful. Thank you, Babette."

Jaq reluctantly agreed. "We check the mouse-size places, and Cinderelly check the princess-size places."

The three mice scurried from room to room. They looked behind curtains, on top of cabinets, and even in the tea room. Gus checked inside an entire tea set.

"Gus-Gus, Cinderelly's bracelet isn't in a teapot," Jaq laughed.

Gus looked embarrassed, but Babette spoke up quietly. "It never hurts to check."

The mice continued searching the tea room until Babette let out a squeal of joy.

"Jaq! Gus! Look!" she cried. Babette had found Cinderella's bracelet stuck between two chair cushions.

"Hooray!" Gus and Jaq cheered.

106

The pair of mice hopped down to help Babette free the heavy bracelet from between the cushions.

"You can tell Cinderelly you found it!" Gus said.

"Oh, I couldn't!" Babette said, blushing.

Suddenly, Jaq and Gus understood why Babette had been so quiet. Babette wasn't a snob. She was just shy!

"Be brave!" Gus said, patting her on the shoulder.

"Cinderelly is the nicest princess ever," Jaq said. "You can talk to her."

The mice found Cinderella looking through her bedroom.

Jaq and Gus gently pushed Babette forward with the bracelet.

"Oh, you little dear!" Cinderella cried. "Did you find my bracelet?"

Babette blushed and nodded.

"Thank you," Cinderella said.

Babette saw that she was surrounded by kind friends. She gathered all her courage, looked Cinderella in the eye, and said, "You're welcome, Princess."

Now that the bracelet had been found, the three mice decided to play together. Gus had a wonderful idea. He grabbed Babette's paw.

"Hide-and-seek!" he squeaked.

The three friends ran off together. They spent the rest of the day playing in the many castle rooms they had explored earlier.

But their fun couldn't last forever. When it was time for Gabrielle to go home, Jaq and Gus were very sorry to say good-bye to their new friend.

"Come back soon!" Gus said.

Babette waved. "I'll miss you!" she said.

Cinderella, Jaq, and Gus walked outside to see the carriage off. When Gabrielle and Babette were out of sight, Jaq turned to Cinderella.

"Babette!" he said. "She's so much fun."

"The best!" Gus chimed in.

"Oh, really?" Cinderella asked with a smile. "She's not 'stuck up' or a 'snob'?"

"We're sorry, Cinderelly," Jaq said.

"That's all right, Jaq," Cinderella replied. "I'm sure you'll be more patient with new friends in the future."

Gus nodded sagely, while Jaq exclaimed, "We sure will!"

Tangled

The Sweetest Day Ever

Rapunzel was having the best birthday of her life. She'd finally left her tower. She and her chameleon, Pascal, had made some new friends—like Flynn, the well-meaning thief, and Maximus, the noble horse. In a few short hours, she'd get to see the floating lanterns she'd always wondered about.

And now they had time to explore the kingdom of Corona. Since today was the celebration of the lost princess's birthday, the whole town was out and about for the festivities.

Rapunzel had never met so many interesting people. There were musicians playing lively tunes, kids drawing with chalk, and all sorts of street vendors selling goodies. Rapunzel found she had plenty to talk about with all of them.

"Hello there!" called a man behind a fruit stand. "Crispy, delicious apples? They're straight from my farm."

Rapunzel bounded up to greet him. "They certainly look delicious," she responded. "What's it like owning a farm?"

Farther down the street, Rapunzel got into a conversation with another vendor. "Wow! Are these your paintings? What types of brushes do you use?"

"I know a fellow artist when I see one," the painter said. The two started chatting like old friends.

Suddenly, Rapunzel and Flynn heard a commotion behind them. The sounds of crashing pans and loud voices erupted from an open window.

"I have half a mind to call the palace guards!" a voice cried.

"Hey! A bakery!" Rapunzel said, noticing the sign. She headed straight for the door.

"Um . . . what was that about 'palace guards'?" Flynn asked. He knew the guards weren't that good at hunting him down, but he didn't want to walk straight to them. "Besides, I don't even like sweets!"

Despite Flynn's protests, Rapunzel followed her curiosity inside. Her attention was immediately drawn to the lively feud in front of her.

"I'm sorry, but we're all out!" said a small man crouching in fear.

"How can you be out on today of all days?" a flushed baker asked the dairyman. "How am I going to make my famous Lost Princess Cupcakes without milk and eggs?"

Rapunzel stepped forward. "Wait, you don't have eggs or milk?"

"That's right," the baker responded, her eyes narrowing at the strange blond girl who'd suddenly appeared in front of her.

"I can help! Stay right there," Rapunzel declared. And with that, she ran out of the bakery as fast as she could.

The baker and the dairyman now turned to stare at the man left standing awkwardly nearby.

"Uh . . . I guess I'll go help," Flynn said, darting out behind her.

First Rapunzel rushed back to the farmer's stand. Flynn, Maximus, and Pascal hurried behind her.

"Hi again, Frank! I need some of your finest!" Rapunzel grabbed as many apples as she could carry.

Then they stopped by the artist's corner. "You don't have any unused paintbrushes you could spare, do you, Felix?" Rapunzel asked.

Soon girl, boy, horse, and chameleon were back at the bakery, their goods in tow.

The baker led Rapunzel into the kitchen, curious about what the girl was going to propose. She was so intrigued she didn't even think twice about the large horse and bright chameleon peeking into her shop.

"You don't need eggs or milk," Rapunzel announced, pulling out some pots and pans from behind the counter. "You can use applesauce!"

"Applesauce?" repeated the baker.

"Yep!" Rapunzel taught the baker her favorite way of whipping up some applesauce quickly.

In no time, golden, fluffy cupcakes were cooling on the counter.

"And now to add a little pizzazz," Rapunzel said. She grabbed one of the borrowed paintbrushes and started to decorate the cupcakes with colorful frosting. The baker inspected Rapunzel's work with admiration.

"You saved the day!" the baker said. "Cupcakes for everyone . . . even you, Lester," she said, eyeing the dairyman. She handed Flynn a basket filled with the beautiful sweet treats.

Rapunzel and Flynn knew just where to take them. Saving the Lost Princess Cupcakes had been a team effort, after all.

Frank loved the sweet taste.

Felix loved the frosting decorations.

"I think I'll try one now, too," Rapunzel said, taking a cupcake out of the basket.

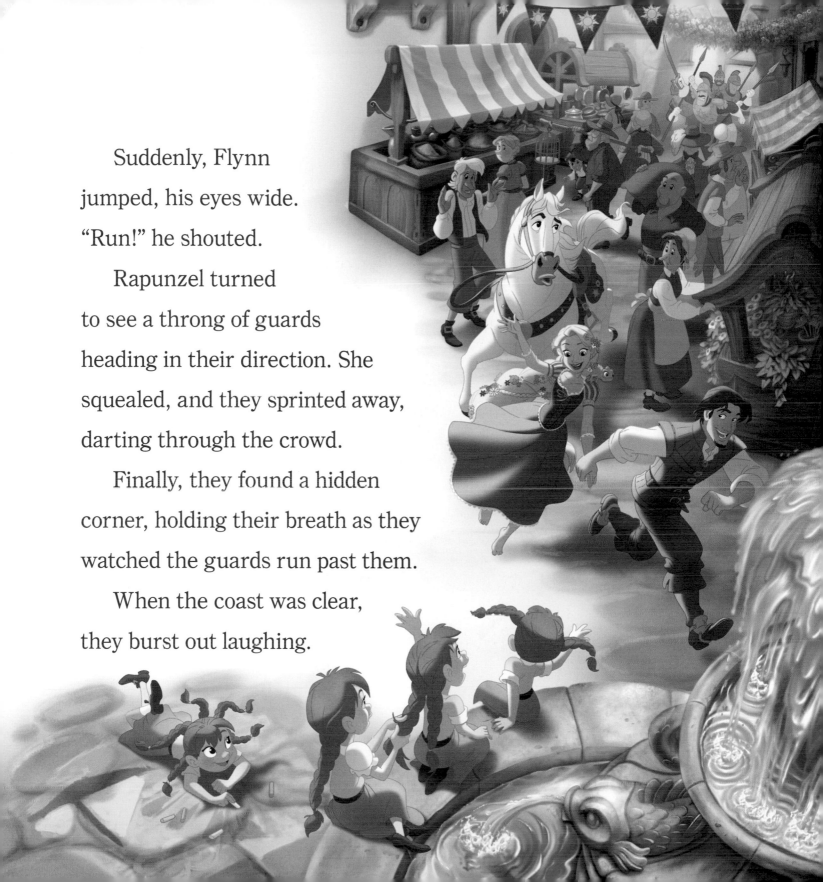

Suddenly, Flynn jumped, his eyes wide. "Run!" he shouted.

Rapunzel turned to see a throng of guards heading in their direction. She squealed, and they sprinted away, darting through the crowd.

Finally, they found a hidden corner, holding their breath as they watched the guards run past them.

When the coast was clear, they burst out laughing.

"I sure have worked up an appetite," Flynn said, grabbing a cupcake from the basket.

"I thought you didn't like sweets," Rapunzel teased.

"I'll make an exception this time," he said, tipping his cupcake toward Rapunzel and taking a bite. "Wow! That *is* delicious."

"Thanks," Rapunzel said, taking a bite out of her own. They looked at each other for a moment. Both felt themselves blushing and grinning.

As the sun started to set, Rapunzel thought about how truly sweet the day had been . . . and it wasn't over yet! Soon it would be time to see the floating lanterns with her best friends at her side.

THE PRINCESS AND THE FROG

A New Chef in Town

Tiana dipped a spoon into a pot of bubbling stew. *Mmmm,* she thought as she took a taste. *Just enough spice!* She made a note in her secret recipe book.

She was working on a brand-new dish at her restaurant. The restaurant was always packed with people who came from near and far to try Tiana's food—especially her gumbo. Tiana hung her apron on its hook. "Time to greet the customers!" she announced as she exited the kitchen.

Tiana went from table to table, saying hello and making sure everyone was happy. Eventually she arrived at a table where one man was sitting alone. "Are you enjoying your meal today?" she asked the man.

The man glanced up. "The okra was satisfactory, the rice was interesting, and the gumbo was . . . disappointing," he told her.

Disappointing? Tiana wondered in surprise. Her gumbo was her best-selling dish!

Tiana walked over to where her friend Charlotte was sitting. She told Charlotte what the man had said.

"Oh, Tia," Charlotte cooed. "That's Leon Robere! He told me he was one of the most famous chefs in the world! I saw him here last week, too. He just opened up a restaurant in town, and— oh! You just must try his gumbo. It's divine."

Tiana looked back at Leon. He was happily eating some beignets. When he saw Tiana, he frowned and put down the beignets.

The next day, the whole town seemed to be buzzing with
excitement about Leon's new restaurant. And Tiana kept hearing
about that gumbo of his. She decided she had to try it.

That night, she and Naveen went to Leon's restaurant.

"Now let's see what all the fuss is about," Naveen said when two
beautiful bowls of gumbo arrived at the table.

Tiana took a bite. Her brow furrowed. She took another bite. Her eyes widened. She took a third bite.

"Wow, this is almost as good as yours!" Naveen said excitedly as he scarfed down the gumbo.

"Naveen," Tiana said calmly. "This isn't *almost* as good as mine. It *is* mine."

Naveen looked up, confused.

"The veggies, the spices, even the way the sausage is cut—it's all exactly the same. Leon copied my recipe!" Tiana whispered to him so no one else could hear. She had to say something to Leon. She decided she would simply tell him that she knew he had used her family recipe. She was sure he would apologize and stop what he was doing.

But Leon did *not* apologize.

"Are you calling me a thief?" he yelled when Tiana confronted him the next day. "I would never use another chef's recipe. Especially not a *bad* recipe!"

Tiana was shocked. What would she do now? Then she had an idea. "Okay . . ." she began. "If you didn't take my recipe, then prove it. I challenge you to a gumbo cook-off tomorrow at noon. No cookbooks or recipes."

Leon paused for a moment. Then he puffed out his chest and said, "Fine! We will cook at *my* restaurant."

That night, Tiana could barely sleep. Word had gotten out about the cook-off, and lots of people would be at Leon's restaurant. What if he hadn't taken her recipe after all? What if his gumbo really *was* better than hers? What if people stopped coming to her restaurant? Her mind raced with questions.

The next day, a huge crowd gathered at the restaurant. In the kitchen, Tiana and Leon faced off. Tiana noticed how tired Leon looked. He must not have slept well, either.

Tiana dashed about the kitchen, grabbing ingredients. She asked Leon where the peppers were, but he didn't answer her.

She couldn't find a good ladle, either.

Then, as she was rushing to the stove, Tiana nearly slipped on some water on the floor.

Daddy would have told me to take my time, she thought. With renewed confidence, she sprinkled some thyme into her pot.

Meanwhile, Leon was having trouble of his own. But Tiana didn't know that. She hadn't noticed when he glanced over to see how many stalks of celery she was using. She hadn't noticed when he used vinegar instead of oil. And she hadn't noticed when he poured twice as much salt into the pot as he was supposed to.

Tiana put the finishing touches on her gumbo. She tasted it. She thought it was good . . . but was it good enough to beat Leon?

The two chefs handed out bowls of gumbo to the hungry people who had gathered. Then Tiana watched as one person

tasted her gumbo and a slow smile spread across his face. She saw another person do the same, and another, and another! And then she noticed something peculiar. Someone else was spitting out Leon's gumbo. Another person looked green in the face. And another person drank an entire glass of water after one bite. What was going on?

"Leon, may I try your gumbo?" Tiana asked the chef.

Leon hesitated. "Uh . . . well . . . if you must," he managed to say, handing her a bowl.

Tiana took a bite and nearly gagged. "I'm sorry," she said, "but what is this?"

Leon shook his head and let out a heavy sigh. "You were right, Chef," he confessed. "I did manage to get ahold of your secret gumbo recipe. I stayed up all night trying to memorize it, but I obviously failed." Leon looked at the floor. "I am very sorry."

Leon explained that when he came to town, all he heard about was Tiana's gumbo. Since he had never cooked gumbo before, he sneaked into her kitchen and found her secret recipe book when he visited her restaurant one day.

Tiana listened to Leon's story. She thought it over for a moment. Leon really did look sorry.

"I have an idea," she said. "I will teach you how to make a basic gumbo. Then you can add some twists to make it your own! In return, you will tell everyone that you borrowed my recipe."

Leon smiled and shook Tiana's hand. "You've got yourself a deal," he replied. "But I have one more favor to ask. Could I have a bowl of your gumbo?"

Tiana laughed. "One bowl of Tiana's Top-Secret Gumbo coming right up!" she said.

BRAVE
The Legend of the Emeralds

Princess Merida raced down the palace hallway. She had looked forward to the Rites of Summer all year long! It was a special festival that celebrated the friendship between the clans. This year, the Macintosh clan would be her family's honored guests. There would be dancing, games, and feats of strength!

At the docks, everyone gathered to greet their visitors.

Young Macintosh stepped down from the boat. The sunlight glinted off a family crest tied to his kilt sash.

"Oh, fancy, are we?" Merida teased him.

Young Macintosh grinned. "What, you don't have a crest of your own?"

"No—but I have this," Merida replied, showing him a lucky charm tied to her bow. "So, shall I beat you at archery or to the top of the Fire Falls first?" she challenged with a sly smile.

"To the Fire Falls!" Young Macintosh cried.

Merida jumped on her horse, Angus, and Young Macintosh followed close behind.

The two reached the base of the Fire Falls at the same time. They began to climb the craggy rocks. They were neck and neck as they approached the top.

Merida pulled herself up. "I won!" she cried.

"Barely!" argued Young Macintosh. Then he looked around. "Wow, this is a fine waterfall you've got here," he remarked. "Where does all this water come from?"

"I'm not sure," Merida replied. "Let's find out!"

Merida and Young Macintosh walked deeper into the forest. Then they stopped short at the edge of a deep lake.

"I suppose this is it," Merida said, disappointed. "I fancied we would have an adventure, but this is just a common loch." She tried climbing a boulder to get a better view. Suddenly, the boulder moved! Merida stumbled forward into a cave, and Young Macintosh jumped up to follow her.

When Merida caught her balance, she gasped at what she saw.

"It's the *real* source of the Fire Falls!" Merida exclaimed, pointing at a pool of glowing water. There, two large, glowing emeralds were resting on a stone ledge. "Those emeralds must be lucky!" she said.

"*Lucky?*" Young Macintosh asked. "But emeralds are a symbol of power, not luck."

"Everyone knows emeralds bring good luck!" Merida scoffed.

Merida and Young Macintosh began to argue.

Suddenly, Young Macintosh snatched up one of the emeralds. "I'm taking this to my father. *Then* you'll see how powerful emeralds are. The Macintosh clan will be stronger than ever!"

"Then I'll be taking the other one!" Merida exclaimed.

They each put an emerald in their own pouch. Neither one noticed that the gems had stopped glowing.

Back at the castle, Lord Macintosh assured them that the emerald was a symbol of power.

"Lord Macintosh is correct," replied Queen Elinor. "But it also symbolizes luck. And we sometimes forget the emerald's most *important* meaning: loyalty. The ancient Legend of the Emeralds is why we're here today." She explained that there used to be fighting between the clans. Then two great kings rose to power, and each placed an emerald at the source of the Fire Falls to symbolize their clans' new friendship. As long as the Fire Falls ran sparkling, there would be peace.

Suddenly, a DunBroch clansman raced into the hall. "The Fire Falls— they've gone dark!" he cried.

Everyone raced outside to look at the lifeless falls. "Who has done this?" cried King Fergus.

Lord Macintosh nodded. "Yes, when King Fergus finds out which one of his DunBroch clansmen did this, he will have my support."

"Which one of *my* clansmen? It was probably one of *your* clansmen," King Fergus said.

The men glared at each other.

"Macintosh clan!" Lord Macintosh commanded. "We're leaving!"

Merida and Young Macintosh looked at each other as everyone else went back to the castle. They *had* to get those emeralds back to where they belonged before the friendship between their clans was ruined! The pair tried to climb up to the cave, but the new, darkened water made the rocks too slippery.

Suddenly, Merida saw a blue will-o'-the-wisp! She knew it would lead them to their destiny. More wisps appeared, drawing Merida's eyes to the top of the falls, where she noticed a small tree.

"If only we had a rope . . ." Merida said.

"You mean, like this?" Young Macintosh asked, showing her a long coil. "I'll throw it up so it twists around that tree," he suggested. But he couldn't throw far enough.

Then Merida had an idea. She picked out her strongest arrow. She pulled back the bowstring, adjusted her aim, and—*whoosh!*—the arrow flew into the sky and landed next to the tree.

Carefully, Merida used the rope to climb the rocks. When she was at the top, she tied the rope to the tree. Young Macintosh followed her up. He was almost at the top when the rope suddenly snapped!

Young Macintosh began to fall, but he grabbed on to a rock just in time. Merida reached out to give him a hand. As she did, her pouch tipped forward, and the emerald she had carefully tucked inside plunged over the cliff!

"No!" Merida cried. The emerald was gone. Merida helped Young Macintosh up.

"You saved my life!" he said. "Thank you."

Merida and Young Macintosh didn't know what they would do, but they hurried back to the cave. The water of the Fire Falls was getting even darker. When they reached the cave, Young Macintosh tried to put the emerald back where he had found it. It nearly toppled off the stone ledge!

Merida looked concerned. "The two emeralds must have supported each other," she said.

What were they going to do without the other stone?

"The legend!" Merida suddenly gasped. "Each king put an emerald on the stone. We've got to put something there, too!" She removed her lucky charm from her bow and placed it on the ledge.

Young Macintosh placed a small knife. For a moment, a sparkling flash crackled and there was a burst of light. But it quickly faded.

Merida shook her head. "It can't just be anything. It has to be something that really, truly matters."

Young Macintosh nodded. He carefully unpinned his family's crest from his kilt sash and placed it on the ledge.

A halo of green light surrounded the objects as they lit up with dazzling sparkles. A golden light flickered out from under the ledge, filling the whole cave.

Then, finally, the water began to glow again! Merida and Young Macintosh raced from the cave just in time to see the Fire Falls turn from black into a clear crystal blue.

From the top of the falls, Merida and Young Macintosh could see the docks. There, clan Macintosh was preparing to leave!

Merida picked out her father, who was standing next to Lord Macintosh. "They're probably still shouting at each other," she said with a heavy sigh.

Quickly, Merida and Young Macintosh raced back down the falls and rode toward the dock.

"Wait!" Young Macintosh called when they were close enough. "We don't have to leave!"

"The Fire Falls are sparkling again," Merida cried. "The water flows as beautifully as it always has!" She explained how she and Young Macintosh had been the ones responsible for ruining the falls—and for fixing them again.

"Now there's no reason our clans can't stay friends," Merida finished hopefully.

"So we don't have to leave?" Young Macintosh asked his father.

King Fergus and Lord Macintosh looked at each other.

"Of course not!" exclaimed Lord Macintosh, smiling at King Fergus.

Merida and Young Macintosh also shared a smile. By working together, they had fixed the Fire Falls—and the argument between their clans. From then on, the Rites of Summer would have a special meaning for both of them.

THE LITTLE MERMAID
Ariel and the Whale Song

"Aaaaariel!" called a voice from beneath the brilliant blue water. Ariel dove into the sea and found her friend Flounder waiting for her.

"Hello, Flounder," she said cheerfully. "Isn't the water lovely today? Oh, you should come up to the surface. The sun feels so nice."

Flounder smiled and shook his head. "I think I'll stay down here," he told Ariel.

"Well, we should get back to Sebastian anyway," Ariel said, pushing her long red hair off her forehead. "I promised him I would sing at the concert today." Sebastian had organized a special concert for the first day of summer. Ariel was sure he'd be setting up for it already. She was also sure that he would *not* be happy if she was late.

Ariel and Flounder swam side by side toward home. Ariel admired the beautiful coral reef as they passed it.

There are always new things to discover in the ocean, she thought. *I wonder if I have time to stop off at the shipwreck before—*

"Ah!" came a shout from behind her. Flounder was quivering and covering his eyes with his fins.

"Oh, Flounder, it's just a little crab," Ariel assured him. She swam over to her frightened friend. "Really, there's nothing to be afraid of!"

She peeled Flounder's fins away from his eyes as the crab scuttled away.

Flounder breathed a sigh of relief.

"We need to toughen you up a bit." Ariel smiled and gently prodded him with her elbow. She loved her friend, but even *she* knew he was a bit of a scaredy-fish.

Ariel and Flounder continued on and finally reached Sebastian, who was leading the orchestra through one of the final songs of the concert. Ariel wasn't *that* late. Why was Sebastian rushing through the rehearsal?

"Sebastian," Ariel said with a laugh, "slow down. We have plenty of time to get ready."

"But Princess, we don't," Sebastian told her. "This isn't just a concert to celebrate the start of summer. It is also a concert we are performing for the *whales*."

"The whales?" Ariel asked.

"Yes. Don't you know? The whales are migrating through Coral Cove today. All of them! And I promised your father this concert would be timed exactly to their passing over us."

Sebastian chattered on, but Ariel had stopped listening. The whales? She would *love* to meet a whale. But how would she meet one if she was singing at the concert?

"And if this concert isn't perfect," Sebastian was saying, "Ariel . . . Ariel?"

Ariel snapped out of her thoughts. "The concert *will* be perfect!" she assured him as she started to swim away.

"Where are you going?" Sebastian cried.

"I just need to get something from my treasure grotto," Ariel said, thinking quickly. "I promise I'll be back before the concert!" And with that she swam off, with Flounder following close behind.

"All right, Flounder.
Are you up for a quick trip
to Coral Cove?" Ariel asked
with a sly smile.

"Coral Cove? But . . .
but why are you going
there?" Flounder asked.

"To meet the whales,"
she told him. "They never
visit us at the palace, so
this is my only chance."

Soon they reached the edge of the reef, where Coral Cove began.

Even Ariel felt a little nervous entering unchartered waters. And was it just her, or had it actually gotten colder?

"I—I don't see any whales here," Flounder stammered.

"Me neither . . ." Ariel added, slightly disappointed. She looked around, hoping to see some sort of sign. But instead of *seeing* a sign, she heard one.

Ariel listened carefully. The noise seemed to be coming from above. The closer she listened, the more it sounded like a song!

"Flounder, follow me!" Ariel said excitedly. She swam quickly toward the brilliant blue light that broke through the ocean's surface. The tune was getting louder. But Flounder noticed a dark shape below them.

Ariel swam all the way up to the water's surface, hoping to find whatever was making the beautiful song. But as she looked around, she saw nothing but the wide, flat ocean.

She frowned, disappointed. "Oh, Flounder. There's nothing here," said Ariel. "And we need to get back for the concert soon or Sebastian will be upset with us. Flounder?" Ariel looked around. Where had her friend gone?

She was about to dive back under when Flounder suddenly burst into the air.

"It was—it was a shark!" Flounder cried. "A shark!"

She tried to calm her friend. "Flounder, sharks don't come into these waters near Coral Cove, remember? It's too close to land for them," Ariel told him. Then she gasped. Something was approaching them, and it sure *looked* like a shark. Ariel dove beneath the waves to get a better look.

It came closer . . . and closer . . . until it was so close that Ariel could make out a giant tail. But before she could figure out who the tail belonged to, it made a giant swooping motion, and an underwater wave surrounded Ariel and Flounder with bubbles!

When the bubbles cleared, Ariel was amazed at what she saw.

It was a mama whale and her baby. And they were singing!

"Whale song," Ariel whispered.

"It's beautiful," Flounder said, amazed—and also relieved there was no shark.

Ariel and Flounder floated next to the whales for a few moments, knowing they might never get this close again. Ariel listened carefully to the melody. Then she sang back to them. The whales smiled at her and continued to sing the tune, and Ariel joined in.

Suddenly, the two whales headed straight toward the ocean's surface and flew into the air. They created a beautiful arc over the water and then belly-flopped onto the smooth surface of the sea. The huge waves sent Ariel and Flounder soaring into the air.

When they landed back in the water, they both had to catch their breath. Then they burst into laughter.

"That was pretty fun!" Flounder cried, still giggling. "Thanks for making me come along, Ariel."

Ariel smiled. It had been an amazing afternoon. But now it was time to get back home.

Ariel and Flounder arrived just in time for the concert. When it was time for Ariel's solo, she decided to make a slight change. She belted out the beautiful whale song she had learned from the

mama and baby whale. Sebastian looked at Ariel in surprise, and Ariel winked at him. As she continued to sing, she could feel the water's currents change, and she knew the whales were passing by. She smiled and sang even louder to celebrate the start of summer *and* to honor her new friends.

Aladdin

The Search for the Sultan's Stone

The sun shone brightly in the sky. Jasmine surveyed the palace grounds. There was still work to do! Tomorrow was the Day of Unity—the day each year when all of Agrabah celebrated the city's history. And this year was the five hundredth anniversary!

Nearby, she spotted her father, the Sultan, speaking excitedly to one of their servants. Jasmine moved closer to listen.

The servant, Farid, shook his head. "I'm sorry, Sultan, but the search party failed to find the stone. The Halari Jungle is just too vast."

The Sultan looked very disappointed. "Thank you for letting me know."

The Halari Jungle? Jasmine thought. She'd always wanted to go there, but her father said it was too dangerous. She found Aladdin and told him what she had heard.

"I bet he was talking about the Sultan's Stone," Aladdin said. "The first sultan of Agrabah was beloved by all. But the sultan's brother was jealous. So he stole an important stone that belonged to the sultan and hid it behind a waterfall in the jungle. No one has ever been able to find it."

"Until today," Jasmine said. "Because *we're* going to find it."

"Sounds like my kind of adventure," Aladdin replied.

He whistled for the Magic Carpet and Abu, and together they took off for the Halari Jungle.

On the way, Jasmine asked Aladdin more about the stone. "What does the Sultan's Stone look like, exactly?"

"Most people believe it's a statue of the first sultan. No one knows what he looked like. I wonder if—"

"That's it!" Jasmine interrupted, pointing to a dense forest in the middle of the desert. "The Halari Jungle!" The Magic Carpet glided to the ground right on the edge of the jungle. Jasmine told the Magic Carpet that they'd return soon.

Jasmine led the way. The jungle was beautiful. It didn't seem scary at all! *Why was Father so concerned about me coming here?* she wondered. *It's so peaceful and—*

"Jasmine, look out!" Aladdin cried.

Jasmine stopped just in time. They were at the edge of a swamp!

Abu squeaked wildly and pointed. Something was moving in the swamp. And not just anything—it was a crocodile!

"Uh . . . maybe we should turn around and try a different route," Aladdin suggested.

But Jasmine spotted just what they needed: two long, strong branches. She handed Aladdin one of the branches. With the other, she vaulted clear over the swamp!

Aladdin used his branch to cross over after her. "Nice work, Princess," he told her. "Now let's find this thing and get out of here."

But after just a few steps, they came to a clearing. In the center was a giant stone covered with beautiful jewels. "Well, that was easy," Aladdin said, giving Jasmine a quizzical look. Could this be the Sultan's Stone? Jasmine started to walk toward the stone, but Aladdin stopped her.

"Jasmine, if the stone is right here, why has no one discovered it yet?" he said. "And I don't see any waterfalls around here."

"Good point," Jasmine replied. "It could be a trap." Instead of walking closer to the stone herself, Jasmine picked a grapefruit from a nearby tree and rolled it to the base of the stone.

ZAP! As soon as the grapefruit hit the stone, there was a blinding burst of light. The grapefruit instantly burned to cinders. Jasmine gasped. "The sultan's brother must have been a powerful enchanter to make a stone do that."

"Well, I'm glad the grapefruit found that out the hard way, and not us!" Aladdin replied.

Jasmine thought the trap must mean they were headed in the right direction. But after hours of searching, she started to wonder if Aladdin had been right. Maybe they *should* have tried a different route to begin with. Everyone was tired, hungry, and ready for a rest. When Jasmine turned around to suggest a break, she saw that Abu had a bunch of berries in his hand. They were a beautiful midnight blue, and they looked exactly like . . .

"Abu!" Jasmine cried as Abu popped a few berries into his

mouth. "Those are Nightbloom berries. They're poisonous!"

Abu squeaked and spit out the berries.

"It's a good thing you didn't eat those, Abu!" Aladdin said. "I know you're hungry. We'll get you dinner soon."

But the berries had gotten Jasmine thinking. Nightbloom berries only grew near water. Jasmine raced ahead, and sure enough, there it was! The waterfall!

Aladdin and Abu caught up. "You found it!" Aladdin cried.

Jasmine and Aladdin walked over to get a closer look. A path of mossy rocks led right behind the falls. Eagerly, Jasmine stepped onto the first rock—and almost slipped into the rushing water!

Slowly, they made it across. But when they reached the back of the waterfall, there was only a bare cave wall! Jasmine sighed. Had they come all this way for nothing? She leaned against the wall to rest. Suddenly, the wall *moved*. "Aladdin, help me push this open!" she exclaimed.

They pushed with all their strength. Slowly but surely, the wall began to turn. When it was fully open, Jasmine and Aladdin saw that there was a secret room!

In the center of the room sat an ancient wooden box. But Jasmine and Aladdin didn't reach for it right away. They remembered what had happened with the stone trap!

Aladdin scanned the room. He took one step forward, lightly placing his foot on the floor. Immediately, the floor tiles began to crumble beneath the pressure. "Jasmine," he said, "are you ready to run? Fast?"

Jasmine nodded, and together they bolted for the pedestal. As the pair ran, the entire floor crumbled behind them! Loose rocks began to fall from above. They dodged left, then right, and just as Aladdin and Jasmine were about to run out of floor, they reached the pedestal.

Instantly, the shaking stopped.

"So, that could have gone better," Aladdin said as he looked at the collapsed cavern behind them.

"At least we have the stone," Jasmine replied, picking up the box. Now empty, the pedestal sank into the ground, revealing a secret passageway.

"Of course! This must be how the sorcerer escaped after hiding the stone," Jasmine said. They followed the passage down and around, left and right, until they emerged back in the jungle on the other side of the waterfall.

"We made it!" Jasmine cried.

"I think it's time to take a look at that stone," Aladdin said.

Jasmine opened the box, expecting to find a statue covered in precious rubies or sparkling emeralds inside. Instead, she found a very simple carving of a woman wearing royal robes. Jasmine turned it over in her hands.

"Look, there's some writing on it," Aladdin pointed out.

Jasmine peered closely at the writing. "'The Stone of Lilah, the first ruler of Agrabah,'" she read. "I guess the first sultan of Agrabah was actually a sultana."

Aladdin smiled. "This is a beautiful statue," he said, admiring it. "And I'm sure Agrabah will be very happy to have it back. Speaking of which . . . *we* should probably get back."

At noon the next day, the people of Agrabah gathered in front of the palace.

"Before we celebrate, my daughter would like to speak," the Sultan announced.

Jasmine stepped forward. "We are so excited to have you at the palace," she began. "And we are even *more* excited because we are celebrating something special on this five hundredth Day of Unity." She thrust the Sultan's Stone into the air. "The return of the Sultan's Stone!" she cried.

The crowd gasped . . . and then broke into wild cheers.

Jasmine glanced at her father, whose mouth was wide open.

"But—but how did you find the Sultan's Stone? I thought it was in the Halari Jungle," he said incredulously.

"It *was* in the jungle," Jasmine said with a smile. "I'll take you there sometime." She winked.

The Day of Unity was a huge success. The people of Agrabah packed the palace grounds, eating, playing, and, most of all, celebrating the return of the Sultan's Stone.

Cinderella

The Heart
of a Champion

One day, Cinderella was visiting her old friend Frou in the royal stable, when her mouse friends Jaq and Gus told her that a messenger had arrived at the palace! Cinderella said good-bye to Frou and the other horses and hurried off to hear the news.

It seemed there was going to be a horse show. The King usually entered it, but he never did very well. Now that Cinderella was part of the family, he thought she would be the perfect person to represent them.

"Why, I'd be delighted," Cinderella said when the King suggested it.

The next thing Cinderella knew, the King was leading her back to the royal stable. The Prince and the Grand Duke went with them.

"The finest horsewoman in the kingdom must have the finest horse in the kingdom," the King said. "I have a stable full of champions, my dear. We'll choose the best of the best, and you can begin training right away. Ah, yes! I can see those blue ribbons already!"

The King ordered his groomsmen to saddle up his horses—all 122 of them—and bring them out to the courtyard.

Cinderella climbed onto the back of the first horse. She knew the stallion was the King's favorite. But he was just a bit too small. The next horse, however, was too big.

Cinderella sat on one horse after another, but none of them was quite right.

Finally, Cinderella dashed back into the stable. "I'll be right back!" she called. "I know the perfect horse!"

Moments later, Cinderella returned, leading Frou!

The King stared at Cinderella and Frou in disbelief.

"Frou may be old," said Cinderella, patting the horse's shaggy mane, "but he has the heart of a champion!"

The first thing Frou did, however, was trip over a nearby water trough. Cinderella flew over his head. She landed in the trough with a splash! The other horses whinnied with laughter, but Frou hung his head.

"Don't worry," Cinderella said to the King. "By next week, we'll be ready."

Cinderella and Frou trained for hours each day.

But Frou kept making mistakes. No matter how sweetly Cinderella urged him, he missed every jump.

And no matter how firmly she steered him, he went the wrong way every time.

"Oh, Frou," Cinderella said, patting his head, "I know you can do it!"

No one else was quite so sure—especially Frou!

Suddenly, Cinderella's fairy godmother appeared.

"I overheard your little mouse friends talking," she explained.

"They said you need a miracle. So, here I am!"

Cinderella laughed and shook her head. "Oh, that's kind of you," she said. "But we don't need a miracle, just a good night's sleep."

"My dear," her fairy godmother whispered, "you know Frou can win, and I know Frou can win, but our friend Frou doesn't believe in himself yet. I'm going to help."

With that, she raised her magic wand and waved it at Frou. Suddenly, Cinderella and Frou had new outfits! A glass horseshoe appeared on each of Frou's hooves!

"With these horseshoes, you'll never miss a step," the Fairy Godmother said.

The next day at the horse show, Cinderella saw more fine horses than she had ever seen before. They all looked like champions—but so did Frou! He held his head up high and stamped his hooves proudly.

The King could hardly believe that Frou was the same horse he'd been watching trip and stumble all week long.

Frou cleared every jump with ease. He never took an awkward step or a wrong turn. He even managed a graceful little bow to the judges at the end of his routine.

Cinderella smiled. Her fairy godmother had been right. Frou had only needed a reason to believe in himself.

In the end, there was no question who belonged in the winner's circle—Princess Cinderella and Frou!

"You know," the King told the Grand Duke, "I had a special feeling about that horse all along. . . ."

After the horse show, Frou returned to his stall at the palace stable with his head a little higher, his back a little straighter, and his glass shoes ready for the next time duty called.

MULAN
Khan to the Rescue

Mulan sighed loudly as she dipped her brush into the pot of ink and gently touched it to the paper in front of her. She hated practicing calligraphy. It was so boring.

Outside, she heard a horse neigh in the distance. Mulan wished

she was out there, too— not stuck inside with the musty ink pot and her own thoughts.

Ignore it, she told herself. *Calligraphy, calligraphy, calligraphy—* NEIGH!

Mulan jumped a mile. Her father's horse, Khan, was standing right outside her window!

Mulan hurried outside. Right away she noticed something alarming!

"That's Grandma's hat," Mulan said to Khan. "And that's Grandma's basket. And now, come to think of it, Grandma was going to take you down to the orchard today. And here you are . . ."

But where was Grandma?

Khan pawed the ground impatiently. Mulan knew he wouldn't have left Grandma alone unless she needed help!

Khan whinnied again and tossed his head back toward the saddle.

"You want me to climb up?" Mulan guessed. "You'll take me to her?"

"I want to," Mulan told Khan, "but I'm not allowed! Wait here, and I'll run into the village and get help."

Khan butted her urgently with his big, soft nose.

"I know," Mulan said, rubbing his ears. Oh, it was so frustrating! Mulan was trying to be a proper lady, and proper ladies did not hop on horses and ride to the rescue.

But maybe just this once . . .

"You're right," Mulan said, making a decision. "There isn't enough time to go to the village."

Just this once.

209

The moment Mulan settled in the saddle, Khan leaped into a full gallop. Mulan held on for dear life as the horse sped through the countryside. They galloped over hills and through valleys. They jumped over fallen trees and splashed through rivers.

Soon they arrived at the orchard, and Khan skidded to a stop in front of an old cherry tree. Mulan slid down from the saddle.

"Grandma?" she called. She looked all around, but she couldn't see her grandmother. "Grandma!"

"Up here!"

Mulan looked up into the branches of the old cherry tree.

"The ladder fell," Grandma said. "And I couldn't climb down. I'm so happy to see you, Mulan!"

"I'll get you down right away!" Mulan promised. But when she picked up the ladder, it fell apart in her hands.

"Oh, no," Mulan said. "The ladder is broken."

Grandma looked worried. "Maybe you should go get help from the village," she said.

"It would take forever," Mulan replied. "Don't worry, Grandma, I've got this."

Mulan looked around. "Okay," she muttered to herself, "let's see what we have to work with. One horse, one saddle, two baskets, one bridle . . . Aha!" She had the perfect plan.

First she unbuckled Khan's reins from his bridle and tied a piece of her sash to them. Then she tied one end of the leather strap to a basket.

Mulan tossed the strap up to her grandmother. "Sling it over the branch," she instructed. Then she tied the other end of the makeshift rope to Khan's saddle. Mulan held Khan's bridle and backed him slowly away from the tree. The strap pulled tight, and the basket rose into the air until it was right next to Grandma!

"Step into your chariot, Grandma," Mulan said with a grin. Once her grandmother was safe in the basket, Mulan led Khan forward step-by-step until the basket was back on the ground.

"You did it!" Grandma cried,
rushing over to hug Mulan.
"You brave girl!"

"Well," Mulan said,
blushing, "not *that* brave. I
mean, I wasn't the one stuck
up a tree."

"You *are* brave," Grandma
said. "Brave and brilliant."

Mulan and Grandma took
their time returning home.
Khan didn't seem to mind—he
paused to graze as they went.

"Father will be angry," Mulan told her grandmother nervously. "I was supposed to be practicing calligraphy today."

Grandma made a thoughtful *hmmm* sound. "I think," she said, "I can help with that. Just this once."

That evening at dinner, Mulan's father asked her how her studies had gone.

"Actually," Grandma spoke up, "I helped Mulan with her calligraphy today."

"Oh?" Mulan's father said. He turned to Mulan. "What character did you practice?"

"The character of 'courage,'" she replied. Mulan and Grandma shared a secret smile. "I had a great teacher."

Tiana and Charlotte's Friendship Fix-up

Charlotte rummaged through her closet. She was looking for the perfect dress to wear to dinner that night, but she didn't seem to like anything she tried on. "I've got nothing new to wear, Tia. We need to go shopping."

Tiana groaned. "I hardly have time to sit, let alone shop, Lottie."

Charlotte pouted. "Oh, you're always so busy with your restaurant and Naveen. We need a friendship fix-up, Tia. I just want to spend time with you."

Charlotte had a point. Tiana had been beyond busy.

"All right," she said. "We can go!"

Charlotte squealed with joy.

First thing, Charlotte led Tiana to the Bayou Boutique and held up a puffy dress. "Isn't this darling?" she said.

"That's swell, Lottie," Tiana replied. "Shall we get it and go?"

But Charlotte wasn't so sure. She tried on dress after dress after dress.

Hours later, Charlotte finally started picking which dresses she wanted.

"Almost done?" Tiana asked hopefully.

"Just one more thing," Charlotte replied, grabbing a dress from her growing pile. "This dress is perfect for you!"

"Me?" Tiana said. "But I love the dresses Mama made for me. I don't need another."

"And I love them, too," Charlotte said. "But there's always room for something new!"

"I don't know, Lottie. . . ." Tiana said.

Charlotte tried and tried to convince Tiana to get the dress, but Tiana refused. Charlotte could tell her friend was starting to get frustrated. This shopping trip wasn't going at all like Charlotte had hoped!

"All right," Charlotte said, dropping the dress. "If you don't want to shop, let's do something else instead." Charlotte thought for a moment, then snapped her fingers. "I know just the thing!"

Charlotte led Tiana to the kitchen of Tiana's restaurant. "I can help you cook!" Charlotte said. "Won't that be fun?"

Tiana wasn't so sure, but she thought she should at least give it a try. Together, Tiana and Charlotte started making the dough for Tiana's signature dish—beignets!

Their first batch was a smashing success. But then Tiana was called away to talk to a customer in the dining room.

"Can you handle the next batch on your own?" Tiana asked.

"No problem, Tia!" Charlotte said. "You can count on me."

After Tiana left, Charlotte rolled out the dough. *These beignets need some pizzazz*, Charlotte thought. She cut each beignet into one of her favorite shapes.

Charlotte placed the beignets into the fryer to cook, then she started on another batch of dough. She hoped Tiana would be back soon. Cooking wasn't nearly as much fun without her best friend.

Charlotte was about to go looking for Tiana when she caught a whiff of something that made her heart skip a beat.

Smoke was pouring of Charlotte's frying pot! She had left the beignets cooking for too long.

Tiana ran in from the dining room. "Lottie! What did you do?"

Charlotte felt terrible for ruining the beignets. This wasn't how she wanted things to go. She started to cry and ran from the kitchen.

Charlotte didn't stop running
until she got home. The day had
been a complete disaster. She
just hoped that Tiana would
forgive her.

Tiana wished she could go after Charlotte, but there was a kitchen to clean and meals to cook for hungry customers.

She got right to work throwing out the burned beignets. Then she saw one of the special beignets Charlotte had made. Tiana's heart sank. She hoped her best friend was okay.

Later that night, both Charlotte and Tiana knew they had to find each other. Charlotte headed over to Main Street, hoping to run into Tiana. Tiana did the same.

In no time, the friends spotted each other.

Tiana ran to Charlotte and hugged her tightly.

"I'm sorry!" Charlotte cried. "My friendship fix-up was a complete disaster."

"I'm sorry, too," Tiana said. "You were just trying to find something fun for us to do together."

"I want to spend time with you, Tia, but maybe shopping or cooking isn't it," Charlotte said.

"I agree," Tiana said. "So what can we do?"

Tiana looked up as if to find an answer— and she did! "Look, Lottie!"

"'The Frog Prince,'" Charlotte said.

"Our favorite!" they said together.

After the show, Tiana said, "That was amazing."

"Oh, yes!" Charlotte smiled. "But the way your mama told the story when we were girls is still the best."

"Thank you, Lottie," Tiana said, giving Charlotte another hug. "This was the perfect friendship fix-up!"

POCAHONTAS
A Little Mischief

Pocahontas was the daughter of the chief of the Powhatan tribe. She knew the woods better than anyone, and she was a friend to the animals that lived around her village, like her hummingbird companion, Flit.

One day, Pocahontas's father went away to visit a nearby tribe. "I'll be back by sundown. I'm putting you in charge, Daughter," the chief said. "Make sure nothing goes wrong in the village."

Pocahontas was honored that her father had trusted her with the responsibility. She was determined to make him proud!

The rest of the morning, Pocahontas was busy in the village. She repaired wigwams, gathered herbs for Kekata the medicine man, and taught the young boys and girls how to track.

By that afternoon, the only thing Pocahontas had left to do was check on the fields. But on her way, she was stopped by Alawa, one of the youngest girls in the tribe. "Pocahontas! A crow took my favorite necklace," Alawa said sadly. "Could you help me get it back?"

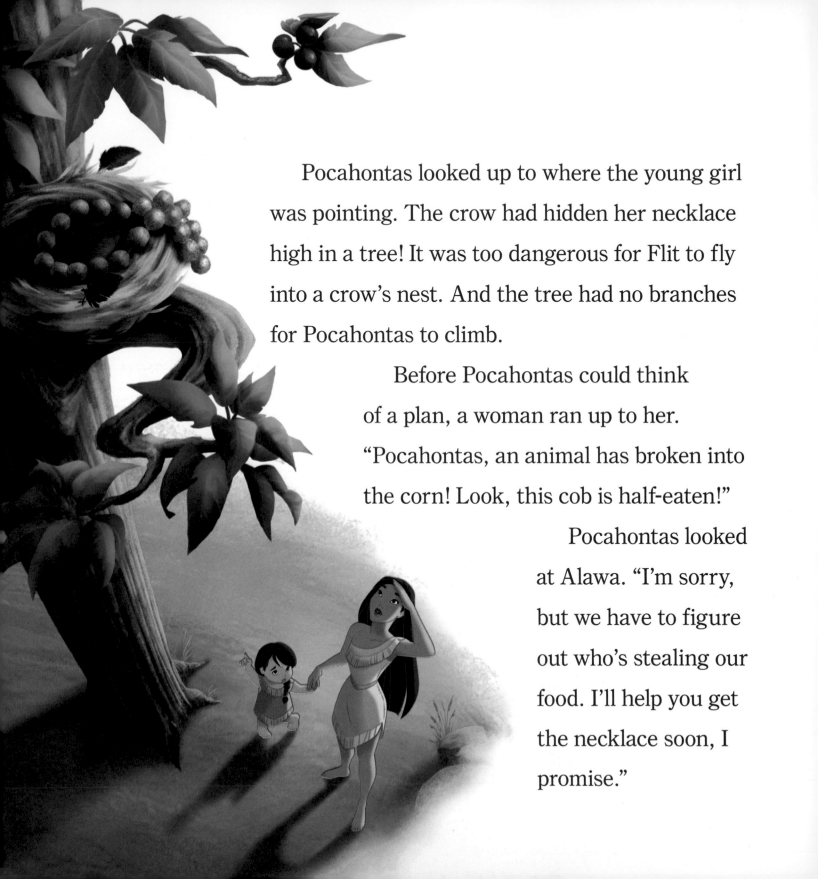

Pocahontas looked up to where the young girl was pointing. The crow had hidden her necklace high in a tree! It was too dangerous for Flit to fly into a crow's nest. And the tree had no branches for Pocahontas to climb.

Before Pocahontas could think of a plan, a woman ran up to her. "Pocahontas, an animal has broken into the corn! Look, this cob is half-eaten!"

Pocahontas looked at Alawa. "I'm sorry, but we have to figure out who's stealing our food. I'll help you get the necklace soon, I promise."

Pocahontas followed the woman to where the tribe stored the corn. "It looks like something has broken through the side of the wigwam. Look, it left a trail!" Pocahontas said.

Together, Pocahontas and Flit followed the trail of corn. It went over logs and under fallen trees. The trail went right by small creeks and past animal dens. But suddenly, the trail of corn stopped in a small clearing.

Flit chirped at Pocahontas. "Don't worry, Flit," she said. "There must be other signs that will tell us where our visitor has gone."

Pocahontas looked around and saw a broken branch on the ground. "Something stepped on this branch to make it break. I think our visitor went this way."

A little farther into the forest, Pocahontas noticed a set of claw prints in the soft earth. And then she saw a little bit of fur on a berry branch. "We must be getting close," Pocahontas said. She soon tracked the visitor to a small den.

"Hello?" Pocahontas called. "I promise not to hurt you. I just want to know why you're taking our corn."

There was no answer. Flit flew inside to get a better look, but before Pocahontas knew it, Flit was zooming back past her. Something had thrown Flit out of the den, and now the poor hummingbird's beak was stuck in a tree!

As Pocahontas pulled her friend free, she saw a raccoon run out of the den and into the woods.

Pocahontas and Flit raced after the raccoon. "You don't need to be afraid!" Pocahontas called, but the raccoon would not stop.

The raccoon reached a bend in the river, but he quickly jumped across a line of stones to the other side. Pocahontas leaped after him. She saw the raccoon run up to the top of a very high tree!

"Please come down," Pocahontas told the raccoon. "We aren't angry that you took our food." Pocahontas held out the half-eaten cob of corn. Slowly, the raccoon crept down the tree. He quickly took the corn from Pocahontas's hands and began to eat it.

"I think you need a name," Pocahontas said. "What do you think about . . . Meeko? It means 'little mischief.' Can I call you Meeko?" The raccoon looked up from the corn and nodded happily.

Pocahontas looked up at the tall tree that Meeko had just climbed. She had an idea, but first they had to go back toward the village.

Pocahontas gestured for Meeko to follow her, but Meeko looked worried. "It will be all right," Pocahontas said. "I know that you were just hungry, and you didn't know it was wrong to take the corn. But I think I know a way that you can help us out."

They walked together until they reached the
bottom of the large tree with the crow's nest.
"Do you think you can get the necklace back for
us, Meeko?" she asked.

Meeko nodded. He'd be glad to help!

Meeko quickly ran up the tree. Then he stretched his paw over the edge of the nest and felt around until he found the necklace. Meeko held it up for Pocahontas to see.

"Good job, Meeko!" Pocahontas called. "Now come down, carefully."

As Meeko began to make his way back down to the ground, Pocahontas heard the cry of an angry crow. The crow swooped

toward Meeko. He wanted his necklace back!

"Hurry!" Pocahontas called. She was too far away to help. Meeko ran down the tree, and just before the crow was about to catch him, the raccoon leaped right into Pocahontas's arms! He was safe!

"You did it, Meeko!" Pocahontas said. The new friends went into the village to find Alawa. When she saw Pocahontas, the girl ran over, excited.

"Did you get my necklace, Pocahontas?" she asked.

"I had some help from my friend here," Pocahontas said. Shyly, Meeko held out Alawa's necklace.

"Oh, thank you!" she cried. She grabbed Meeko and gave him a big hug.

As the sun began to set, Pocahontas saw her father's canoe pull up to the shore. She ran to greet him, with Meeko following close behind.

"How did you fare today, Daughter?" he asked. "I hope there wasn't any trouble."

"Nothing we couldn't handle," Pocahontas said, smiling. "Right, Meeko?"

"Ah, just a little mischief, then?" Pocahontas's father returned her smile.

"Exactly."

The light was fading, and Pocahontas knew it was time to say good-bye to Meeko. "Stay safe," Pocahontas said as they walked toward the woods. "And stay out of the corn, too!"

Meeko started to climb a tree, but then he paused and turned back to Pocahontas.

"Yes?" Pocahontas asked with a smile. Meeko ran back to Pocahontas and leaped into her arms. Pocahontas laughed. "Don't worry, we'll see each other again. I can visit you in the woods anytime."

Meeko looked up at her happily. "And I can bring you any extra corn when I do," she added.

Meeko liked the sound of that!

Beauty and the Beast
The Friendship Invention

"Oh, Papa, isn't it exciting?" Belle asked. She and her father, Maurice, were walking toward the center of town. It was the day of the first annual Invention Convention. Maurice had been organizing it for months. And the big day had finally arrived!

"It certainly is," said Maurice. "People from all over the countryside are coming. I have a feeling there are some big surprises in store!"

When Belle and her father arrived, the town square was bustling with more activity than ever before! Townsfolk were eagerly setting up booths to present their incredible inventions.

"Why don't you go and explore while I get ready?" Maurice said.

Belle could hardly wait. She loved seeing new inventions. And there were so many on display!

Everywhere Belle looked there was a new imaginative contraption. Some had lots of bells and whistles. Others were quite practical. Some were simple and sweet.

Just when Belle thought she'd seen it all, she spied a crowd gathered across the square. Belle squeezed through the thick circle of people to see what everyone was oohing and ahhing over.

There must be something extra exciting over here, Belle thought.

When she reached the center, Belle's eyes grew wide. In the middle of the circle was an invention unlike any of the others. And the inventor was a girl Belle's age! She was just about to demonstrate how her machine worked, and she was looking for a volunteer.

"What's your name?" the girl asked Belle.

"I'm Belle."

"My name is Simone. Would you like to be my volunteer?" Simone guided Belle over to her invention. "Please place these leaves on the screen."

Belle did as she was asked. Then Simone closed the flap on the machine and pushed a button.

"*Et voila!*" cried Simone.

Out popped one smooth little piece of paper. Simone's invention pressed tree leaves into paper! The crowd applauded.

As the people left, Belle helped Simone collect her pile of leaf paper.

"How did you think of such a clever invention?" Belle asked.

"When I was little, I always wanted to build an invention that could spread happiness," Simone explained. "One day I realized special notes make people happy. Sometimes you even make a new friend with a note. So I decided to invent a machine to create paper as special as the notes."

Belle looked at the stack of beautiful leaf paper. "That gives me a fantastic idea!" she said.

Simone look down at the paper, confused.

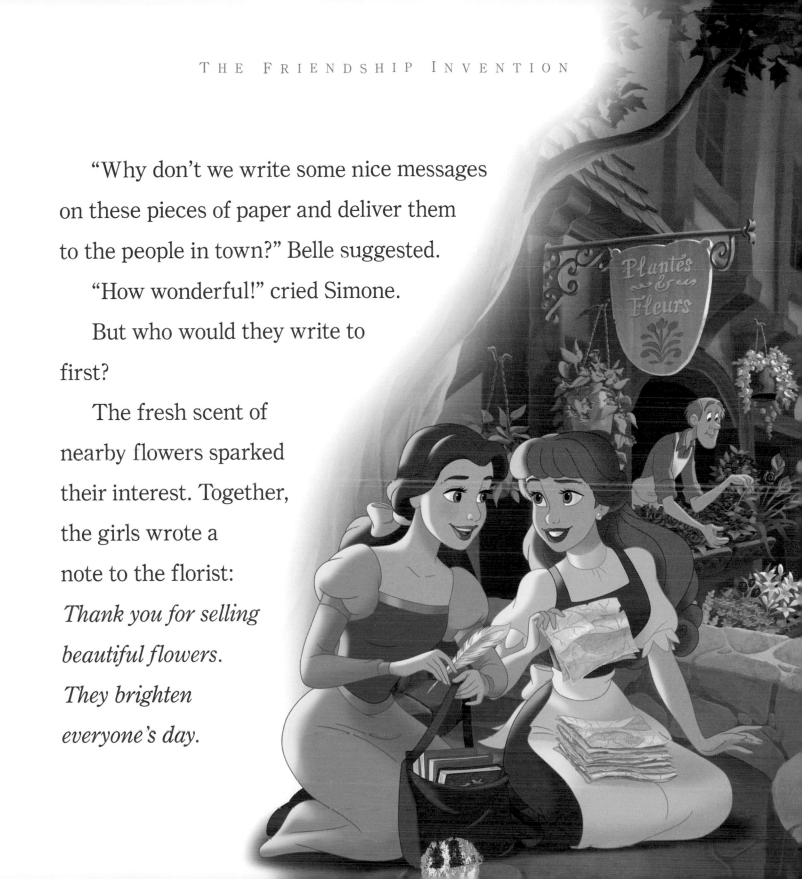

"Why don't we write some nice messages on these pieces of paper and deliver them to the people in town?" Belle suggested.

"How wonderful!" cried Simone.

But who would they write to first?

The fresh scent of nearby flowers sparked their interest. Together, the girls wrote a note to the florist: *Thank you for selling beautiful flowers. They brighten everyone's day.*

Belle and Simone delivered the note, but they didn't sign it. They wanted to spread happiness in secret—that made it more exciting.

They watched as the florist opened his message. Reading it seemed to make him very happy!

"This is fun!" said Simone. "Let's write another one."

"Who should we write to next?" asked Simone.

Hmmm, Belle thought. "How about the bookseller? His books always make me happy. I think a nice note would be the perfect way to say 'thank you.'"

So Belle and Simone wrote a note to the bookseller . . .

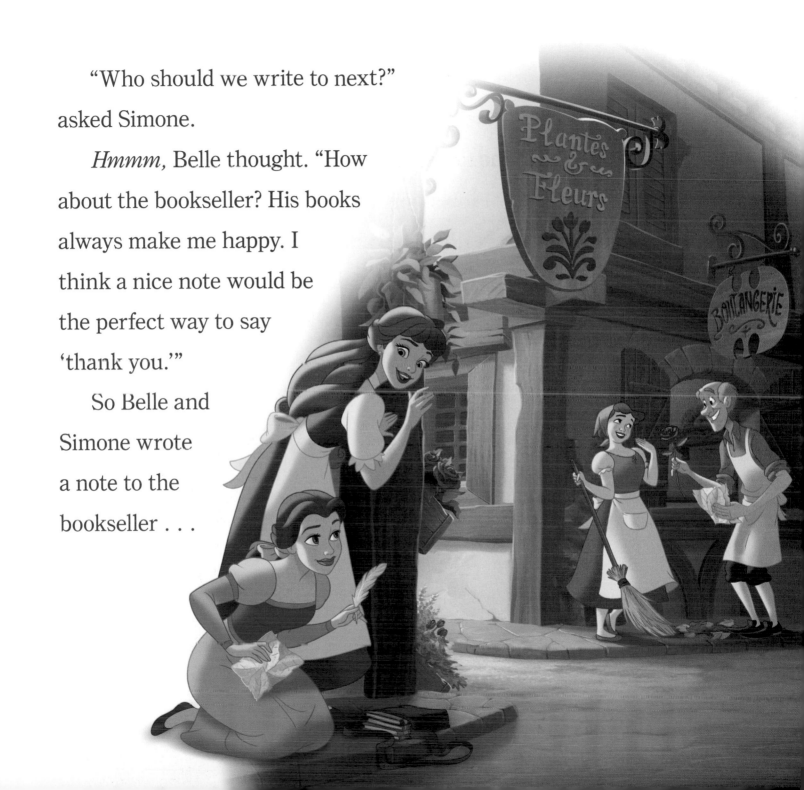

. . . and delivered it in secret!

The bookseller was with a customer when he discovered it. Belle and Simone watched as he opened it, read it, and smiled.

Belle winked. "Your invention is working!" she whispered to Simone. "It really is spreading happiness!"

Together, the girls delivered nice messages to many of the townsfolk. Soon they had only one sheet left.

"Who should we write our last note to?" Simone asked.

"I know just the person," said Belle.

A short while later, Belle and Simone delivered a very special handwritten message to Maurice. This time, they did not hide.

Dear Papa,

Thank you for organizing this wonderful convention. It brought two new friends together. —Belle and Simone

Maurice chuckled. "You're quite welcome." Then he handed the girls new books. "The bookseller asked me to give these to you. He recognized your handwriting, Belle, and wanted to thank you. The note made him very happy."

At the end of the day, the convention was over. It was time for Simone to pack up her invention and say good-bye.

"I had a wonderful time," Simone told Belle. "I'm so glad we met. And I wanted to give you this." She handed Belle a beautiful fresh stack of leaf paper. "Promise you'll write?"

Belle hugged Simone. "Of course," she said. "And you must write me back. I want to hear about all the incredible new inventions you come up with!"

Belle waved as Simone's cart rolled away.

She was going to miss her new friend.

But later that night, when Belle opened her new book, she was surprised to find a special note from Simone tucked inside. And when she read it, she knew their friendship would last.

Belle couldn't wait to see Simone again. She was sure their next adventure would be even more fun.

Sleeping Beauty
A Moment to Remember

Princess Aurora sighed. She loved being married to Prince Phillip, but life in the palace was so different from what she was used to. Now that she had moved away from the humble cottage in the forest, it seemed all she did was plan and attend parties. That night there would be yet another royal ball, and everyone was fussing over the plans.

The royal florist and the table setter couldn't agree on flowers. "Princess Aurora," said the royal table setter, "could you please tell

the royal florist that our guests will never see one another if I put his big flower arrangements in the middle of each table?"

"Why don't you just put a single flower on each table?" Aurora suggested.

The two servants looked at her, horrified at her simple suggestion.

Just then, Prince Phillip entered the room. "Good after—" he started.

"Pardon me, Princess Aurora," the royal steward interrupted, "but I must have your approval on the seating arrangements."

"Thank you," said the princess. "I will look at them—"

"As soon as we return," Prince Phillip finished.

Both Aurora and the steward looked at Phillip in surprise.

"Where are we going?" Aurora asked.

Phillip smiled. "Out for a ride in the forest—by ourselves."

Aurora was delighted. It was just what she had been hoping for. The princess hurried to change into her riding outfit.

273

But as the couple started to leave the stable, the royal equestrian guards insisted they escort the prince and princess. "Who knows what dangers could be out there!" the head of the guards said.

Aurora knew that the forest was perfectly safe, so she leaned down and whispered to Phillip's horse, Samson. The horse whinnied and charged away from the palace.

Aurora's horse, Buttercup, galloped after them. Before long, the guards were far behind.

"Whooaa! Whoa, Samson!" the prince shouted as his horse raced ahead.

"It's all right, Phillip!" Aurora called. "We'll slow down as soon as we lose the guards."

They galloped into the forest, and Samson found a path through the trees. The horse followed it for a while, then stopped very suddenly. Phillip sailed over Samson's head and landed in a stream.

"No carrots for you, boy!" Prince Phillip scolded his horse. He looked up and saw Aurora trying to hide a smile. He grinned.

"Do you remember this place?" Aurora asked.

Phillip waded out of the stream and looked around the clearing. He pulled off his boots and dumped the water out of them. Then he set them in the sun to dry.

Aurora took off her shoes, too. She spun around gracefully, humming a tune.

"Yes," Prince Phillip said softly. "I remember this place. This is where we first met. I heard you singing sweetly, and then we danced together for the first time."

"I will never forget that day," said Aurora, "no matter how busy we get with our royal duties."

Phillip and Aurora smiled, wishing they could bring the peacefulness of the glade back to the palace. Phillip picked a flower and handed it to Aurora.

Aurora took the gift and beamed.

After a beautiful afternoon together, Aurora finally said, "We should go back and get ready for the ball."

"You go ahead, dear," Phillip said. "I'll be back soon."

Aurora nodded and smiled. Their walk had given Aurora an idea for the ball that night. She couldn't wait to surprise Philip.

Meanwhile, Phillip had an idea of his own. "Not a word of this to the princess," he said to her animal friends as he began to gather some flowers.

At the castle, Princess Aurora worked on Phillip's surprise for the rest of the afternoon. Servants moved tables, laid tablecloths, and gathered flowers. Flora, Fauna, and Merryweather flitted about, helping wherever they could.

More than once, Aurora heard a servant murmur, "Our guests will certainly be . . . surprised."

Aurora just smiled. "It is Prince Phillip I want to surprise," she said. "Not a word of this to him."

That night, Aurora had just finished getting dressed when Prince Phillip came into the room. He held out a simple crown he had made from forest flowers. "Would you like to wear this, too?" he asked.

"Oh, Phillip!" Aurora put on the flower crown and hugged him. "It's perfect for this evening. What a lovely gift!"

Aurora took Phillip's hand. "Now I have a surprise for you!" She led the prince down the stairs and into the palace courtyard.

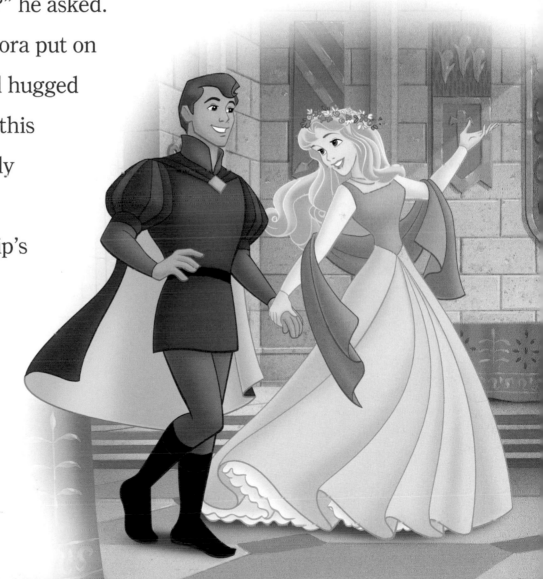

The courtyard was decorated with flowers and trees. Water danced in the fountain. Aurora's woodland friends were there, too.

"The glade will always be in our hearts," Aurora whispered. "But now it is in our palace, too."

Just then, King Hubert came over. "This is much better than the stuffy balls I usually attend," he said to Princess Aurora.

Aurora smiled at Phillip, and they began to dance. Like the first time they had met, this would be a moment to remember.

THE LITTLE MERMAID
Ariel's Royal Wedding

Princess Ariel had loved Prince Eric from the moment she first saw him, even though she was a mermaid and he was a human. And Eric had loved Ariel from the moment he heard her sing. The pair had faced terrible trials to be together. But now that was all behind them. They were finally getting married!

They announced their engagement
with a royal parade. People from all
over the kingdom came to see their
new princess.

Ariel had never been to a human wedding before, so she had a lot to learn. While in the village, she had overheard that human couples dance at weddings. Ariel wanted to surprise Eric with a beautiful dance, so she asked Grimsby to teach her something new.

Grimsby was busy getting the castle ready for the wedding, but he always had time for Ariel.

"One, two, three; one, two, three," Grimsby said as he instructed Ariel in a minuet. Before long, she was twirling across the floor like an expert.

"Well done, Princess," Grimsby said. "You will look so elegant, dancing in your wedding dress."

"Wedding dress?" Ariel asked.

Grimsby suggested that Carlotta would be the best person to ask about a wedding dress. When Ariel found the housekeeper, she had lots of questions. "What does a human wedding dress feel like? Is it hard to walk in?"

"Human wedding dresses are usually flowing and white— and always beautiful!" Carlotta said excitedly. "We can design something that's just right for you, dear."

Ariel and Carlotta got to work, sketching one dress idea after another. Ariel loved the soft white fabric Carlotta suggested, but something was missing.

"Could we add some green here and here?" Ariel asked, pointing to one of Carlotta's sketches. "I want to have something that reminds me of the sea."

"Perfect," Carlotta replied. "I'll take this design to the royal dressmaker right away." She began to leave the room but paused in the doorway. "I promise you will have no problem walking in it," she told Ariel with a smile. "You'll just have to be careful not to get any cake on it."

"Cake?" Ariel asked.

The next morning, Ariel visited Chef Louis in the kitchen. He was busy preparing the wedding menu and baking sample wedding cakes.

"Chef Louis, I don't know what a proper human wedding cake is like," Ariel admitted.

"Don't worry, madam," he said. "I will bake you the most delicious, most exquisite wedding cake in all the land and sea! What flavor would you like it to be?"

"Chocolate!" Ariel said without hesitation. Then she added, "And maybe it could have sea-salt caramel filling?" Sea-salt caramel had always been one of her father's favorite treats.

The wedding plans were almost finished. Ariel found Grimsby to see if there was anything else she could help with.

"All that remains is the guest list," Grimsby said, pulling out a giant roll of parchment.

"Why is the list so long?" Ariel asked in surprise.

"A wedding is for the family as much as it is for the bride and groom," said Grimsby.

That made Ariel think about her own family. Because they all lived under the sea, she had assumed that they wouldn't be able to come to the wedding. And yet in all her preparations she saw things that reminded her of them.

Ariel went back to her room to think. As she considered all the wonderful wedding plans, she remembered what Grimsby had told her: a wedding is for family. It was Ariel's dream to spend the rest of her life as a human, but she still wanted to honor her past as a mermaid. Most of all, she wanted her family close by on her wedding day. She began to feel sad.

Later Eric found Ariel alone on the balcony, looking out at the sea. He noticed tears in Ariel's eyes.

"What's the matter?" he asked.

"I want a human wedding, but I just wish—I just wish that my family could be there, too."

"Ariel, we don't have to have the wedding at the palace," Eric said softly.

"Of course!" Ariel exclaimed. "We can have the wedding at sea on board your ship. Then everyone, both humans and merfolk, can come."

"I wouldn't have it any other way," Eric said, hugging Ariel tightly.

"After all," Ariel added, "that ship is where I first saw you."

Together, Ariel and Eric found Grimsby and told him all about their new plans for the wedding.

The morning of the wedding finally arrived. Carlotta helped Ariel put on her wedding dress.

"It's beautiful," Ariel said. "I just know this day will be everything I hoped it would be."

Together, Ariel and Carlotta made their way to the wedding ship, where everyone was waiting for them.

The human guests were all seated on the deck. The merfolk looked on from the sea. Ariel's father used the magic of his trident to lift him and her sisters up to the side of the ship. Everything was still. Then the music began to play, and Ariel walked down the aisle to Eric's side.

The vows were made. The rings were exchanged.

"Go ahead! Kiss the girl!" cried Sebastian.

And at last, the prince and princess were married!

After the wedding, everyone celebrated together. Chef Louis brought out the wedding cake—chocolate with sea-salt-caramel filling. He had even made a special second cake just for the mer-guests.

As Eric was enjoying his last bite of cake, Sebastian directed the sea animal orchestra to start playing.

"I have a surprise for you," Ariel said happily. She took Eric's hand and began dancing just like Grimsby had taught her.

They were soon joined by other human couples, and merfolk began dancing together in the ocean.

Eric and Ariel's wedding day was a celebration for both land and sea—the beginning of a life filled with joy and laughter, shared with family and friends of all kinds. As the couple waved good-bye to their guests, Eric and Ariel knew this was a day they would remember forever.